A PAPI

The Political Thriller

Penned By

Malcolm Jones

Malcolm is an author with a keen interest in politics.

An apprenticeship served artisan; he became involved with trade unions at eighteen, becoming one of the UK's youngest Shop Stewards.

A thirst for knowledge led him to study politics, sociology and anthropology at City College and the University of Southampton.

Combining his experience as an ordinary British labourer and political campaigner he has developed a unique consciousness of the democratic system we live under.

Conditions of sale

This book is sold subject to the condition that it shall not, by way of trade or otherwise, be lent, re-sold, hired out or circulated without the authors prior consent in any form, binding or cover other than for which it was published and without a similar condition including this condition being imposed on the subsequent purchaser.

Prologue

The scene is an overcrowded Great Britain,
with housing stock full, pollution rising and
living costs out of control.

The government has decided to introduce a
sinister approach to the future as we follow a
group of Southampton dockers during these
challenging times.

Welcome to a Paper Rose.

EPISODES

Episode 1 - Meet the Peeps

Jason wandered through Southampton's
streets, turning his collar to the wind he tilted
his head to light a cigarette - taking a long
draw he exhaled a cloud of smoke that was
briskly whisked away by the oncoming
breeze. In the distance the Ship Inn beckoned
this parched dockworker who'd just endured
another twelve-hour shift.

Quickening the pace, he increased his stride and marched onwards with the thought of a long cold beer diluting the tiredness in his legs.

As the door swung open Nick shouted - 'Oi, Oi here's the gobbler, finally finished hitting the overtime then Jase? Come on son you've some catching up to do.'

Jason headed towards the bar - 'Cheers fella, reckon I've earned this one' putting an arm around his mate he was clearly pleased to be away from work for a change, his face had become weathered over the years, with hands scarred and worn. On the other hand, Nick worked in the office, received a salary, and finished promptly each evening - preferring the pub to life on the docks.

The place was heaving, creating a great atmosphere - it seemed like half the town was in there. Jason and Nick left the bar, moving to a large rectangular table by the juke box and taking up their usual stools.

Seated at the head, sixty-three-year-old Trev was the eldest of them all - since his wife died he'd developed a penchant for whisky which unfortunately led him to be late to work three times in the past week, Jimmy the works foreman was a decent bloke who had a great deal of respect for Trev and wouldn't like to see him sacked, a former union rep he'd managed to hide these indiscretion's from the management.

Finn, the new Trade Union Shop Steward was of Irish descent, having moved to England five years previous he still maintained a strong accent. Getting to his feet the brute of a man revealed a bulky, physically fit figure in excess of six feet with biceps like boulders and stomach as tight as a drum.

Sporting a big red bushy beard and eccentric to the core Finn raised his hat as he strode towards the bar - 'want a beer Jase me old mucker?' he questioned accidently nudging a scruffy looking mush a little worse for wear who immediately quipped - 'watch it, you great big Irish lump, you need to get your sorry arse out of here, climb on your pony and trap then take your two scruffy dogs and huge sack of potatoes back to the campsite.'

Standing in Finns shadow he belatedly remembered his mother's immortal words -

'Son, put your brain in gear before your stupid mouth.'

With the statement still ringing in his ears and desperately seeking succour he turned to his mates with a grimaced half grin shakily forming. Almost immediately a huge fist swung into the side of his face, a streak of spit flew from his now miss-shaped mouth whilst a handful of teeth became strewn across the floor as though someone had dropped a packet of Tic Tac mints, his body quickly followed the dental array crashing to the floor in an untidy heap.

Towering over the silent drunk Finn grunted - 'look maggot, before you start quoting stereotypes don't forget to consider them all, you missed the one about us being bare knuckle fighters you ignorant scrote, here's another cliché - mines a Guinness landlord'.

As he turned barwards the crumpled man's group of friends looked away from the Irish warrior's gaze rapidly losing any will to become involved in an altercation after watching their comrade felled with a single strike.

Sitting back down with a glass in one hand and frothy moustache across his lip Finn re-joined the group with all previous activities seemingly going unnoticed, although more likely there was a sensible lack of interest in challenging the Herculean hulk who was built like a brick house. On his left were two new apprentices who'd started the previous week, at eighteen they were a little shy when it came to conversation, equally so when it came to getting a round in.

The duo sat on a blue velvet bench with a pair of lightly sipped lagers sat in front of them, whilst they stared into their smartphones playing the part of a stereotypical teenager. Jason leant forward, shouting loudly over the music to make himself heard - 'come on lads get your faces out of them screens, into your pints, and join the conversation - you ain't gonna pull any birds if they can't see your handsome chops.' They briefly looked up in unison as if joined at the neck, smiled meekly then returned to their media streams.

Sat quietly next to them was Billy, another apprentice but this one in his early twenties, after spending half a decade in further education he'd decided to earn some cash in the dockyard. Billy's parents had died when he was young leaving him to be raised by his uncle, a reclusive Comicon fan married to his childhood sweetheart whose feline fetish had famously given her the feint aroma of urine and tuna.

They were a well-meaning couple who'd left their nephew to his own means. Learning from university, the internet and life itself he'd developed a rounded understanding of the world whilst avoiding his Aunties strange scent through living in a fully serviced caravan at the end of her garden.

Attempting to start a conversation Trev asked everyone if they'd seen the news earlier, several middle managers and their families had gone missing in the past week, and nobody seemed to know anything about it. 'Not another conspiracy theory Trev' Jason grumbled - 'No its true, people keep disappearing but there's not a lot about it in the media' Trev responded defensively.

Billy looked up and said 'yeah, I saw it on the web this morning 365 missing apparently all linked to middle management, and that's just London' - there was a delay within the group, probably to do with the shock of the shy man's utterance rather than the content of his statement.

Nick asked - 'but whys it not in the media then?' Billy looked up again and muttered 'it's on the web mate, have a look on your smartphone, I'll find a video clip for you.' After a pause Billy passed his phone over, a reporter was interviewing several distraught relatives failing to hold back tears as they told of their missing loved ones - a woman in a pretty-floral dress pulled back her vivid purple hair with tattoo drenched hands as she stated - 'my Husband went missing three days ago and I've not seen him since, the Police haven't been any help, and my kids haven't stopped crying.'

The report continued with a stout balding man stroking his hair island as he told of his sister's family who'd disappeared in similar circumstances.

Nick showed Jason - 'what do you reckon mate?' but he got an immediate response -

'total crap mate, we know the Police spend most of their time sat in their BMW's eating Maccy D's and nicking motorists doing 3mph over the speed limit - even they would know if there was a serial killer knocking off 365 members of the public? You gotta be kidding fella.'

With that Trev changed the subject completely - 'mines a scotch Jase, get your round in you tight arse.' This was going to be a long night.

EPISODE 2 – The Hangover

The sun crept through a crack in the curtains

lighting up Sarah's lovely brown hair, she was

laying on her side staring at her husband who

looked pained as he tried to turn his pillow to

take comfort from the cold side. Hungover

and dry mouthed an eye slowly opened to reveal the distain in his wife's eyes.

'Morning Love' he croaked, the headache providing a firm reminder of his indiscretions last night. He paused, then slowly sat up looking the worse for wear, 'sorry darling, I got a bit carried away with the lads, you know how it goes....'

Sarah raised her eyebrows before offering her little soldier a cup of tea - 'yes, please' he whimpered, sinking into his pillow, and curling into the foetal position.

Ten minutes later a steaming hot beverage arrived followed by a question - 'aren't you supposed to be at work today, Mr Bailey?'......he lay there for a minute before replying - 'I think I'd better stay in bed; not sure I would pass the Drugs & Alcohol test to be fair.'

Since the crane crash last month his employers had been rightly concerned about drugs and alcohol consumption amongst employees with several incidents being attributed to workers under the influence - however, they hadn't bothered to look at the cause – long hours and physical exhaustion.

Smiling to himself Jason remembered an earlier conversation with Dave, 'since they've introduced zero tolerance, I've gone mad for fruit pastels and orangeade to give me a sugar rush and get me through the shift' - Jase let out a little giggle before immediately regretting it as the headache reminded him to stay still.

Jason comforted himself with the thought that he was doing the right thing by staying home - 'safety first' he said to himself whilst turning over and snuggling into the duvet.

An hour had passed before he wandered downstairs to the sound of Milly, his four-year-old scampering up the hallway. Scooping her into his arms he was happy to have a day away from the docks and looked forward to spending some time with his family (besides which tomorrow was Friday, and he could make up his losses on the weekend with a bit of overtime).

Sitting at the dining room table Jason and

Milly made paper roses, carefully folding a

single strip of white paper the young girl

hummed a tune whilst poking her little tongue

out the corner of her mouth to aide

concentration.

'Daddy' she asked - 'how do you know how to

make these flowers?'

'My Mum taught me when I was your age, we didn't really have much money but the simple pleasures in life and spending time together seemed much more valuable than a few quid in the pocket, you can't buy family and you can't purchase love that's why we spend so much time with our precious Milly who, might I add is doing a lovely job of making that beautiful flower.'

'I'm making this for you Daddy, I love you and Mummy - so perhaps I will make her one too.' Standing on the chair she gave Dad a big hug, before sinking her face into his neck, blowing a big wet raspberry, and pulling away giggling excitedly.

'I love you too my little monkey, I'm glad I didn't go to work today - I get to see more of you and Mummy.' Milly snuggled back in - 'me too Daddy, why can't you work a two-day week and have a five-day weekend, it's sad that we can't spend more time together.'

'That sounds like a great idea, maybe you should go into politics, I'd vote for you.' Jason replied smiling.

'Yeah, but you're biased Mr Bailey' said Sarah from across the room.

After eating their lunch, the trio decided to go for a nice walk. Mayflower Park had always been a favourite haunt, a mix of children's play area, fishing from the quayside and watching the cruise liners departing on their international voyages.

The Baileys walked towards the swings, Milly straining at her Daddies hand eager to escape and encourage him to push her higher and higher as she squealed with excitement. It was an idyllic day, and the family felt blessed with the life they had; Jason was remorseful for bunking off but treasured every moment he had with his family.

Trev had always said to him 'life's too short son, ensure you live it to the full and make the most of the time with your kid, it don't last forever.......'

'SPB, SPB, SPB' Milly shouted as her Daddy pushed the swing back and fore, this was the families code for 'Swings, Pies, Bath' which meant a trip to the Pie Shop must be next on the agenda. Milly was only young but had already acquired a taste for chicken Balti pies, a personal favourite of her doting father.

An hour later the family walked briskly up the high street trying to avoid getting drenched by the rain, a change in the weather certainly wouldn't dampen their spirits as they hurried towards Pressley's Pies. The sweet odour of

chicken Balti, leek and potato, Moroccan vegan and steak pies wafted through the air as they came longingly within their grasp.

Pressley's was set back from the main road with a pedestrian area out front, Sarah hugged Milly as they sheltered under a tree whilst Jason popped inside to purchase their special treat.

In the distance a shrill siren blasted from an emergency vehicle, Milly started to copy the noise as the sound of racing engines grew closer and closer, her adoring mother was still looking down at her giggling daughter when a large 4x4 jumped the kerb followed by a matt black unmarked van with sirens wailing.

The escaping driver had lost control and was hurtling towards the pair, Jason turned round hollering at his family to get out of the way just as the jeep smashed into them crushing the startled pair against the tree.

The sound of screaming rang out momentarily as their bodies crumpled, Milly and Sarah were compressed into the rugged bark looking forlornly towards Jason as all life drained out of them.

The occupants of the van jumped out, two of them intercepted Jase who'd launched himself forward lashing violently as he tried to free himself and get to his bloodied family. One of the heavily armed men pulled out a Bazer, (a mix between a riot stick and a taser) forcing the electric current into Jason's back before aggressively beating him around the knees causing the distraught father to hit the floor convulsing and crying out in agony.

Their colleagues had reached the 4 x 4 and were dragging a man, his wife and three children from the wrecked vehicle, having cuffed them they threw the quintet into the waiting van and shouted 'we're done here, let's get ourselves gone' - with a final savage poke of the Baser they all fled the scene, disappearing as quickly as they came.

A crowd had appeared and helped Jason to his feet - as he stumbled over to the carnage Jase began sobbing uncontrollably, his whole life had been ripped apart before him - 'Sarah, Milly, why.... why the hell has this happened, who were those sick bastards...?'

Taking Sarah's hand, he knelt before her staring in disbelief.

With emotions turning to intense anger, he formed a tightly clenched fist growling - 'I promise you darling, I'm gonna kill them all, if

it's the last thing I do.........every, last one of

them, every, last one.

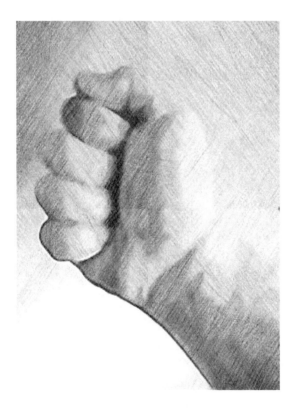

EPISODE 3 – The Funeral

Jason opened the door of the registrar's office in Bugle Street, posters covered the wall providing information on dealing with death, mental health, and financial issues. He sat on a worn wooden seat waiting to be called, looking tired and dishevelled he was struggling with the previous day's events.

With a wandering mind the scene outside Pressley's came flooding back, his darling wife and child pressed against the tree covered in blood, their faces shocked and pained, the black van hurtling off into the distance as he helplessly stared at the

25

carnage. He woke with a start as a hand lightly touched his shoulder - 'Mr Bailey' a voice said softly, 'Mr Bailey, we are ready for you now, would you like to come through?'

He stood up slowly, the vision still buzzing round his head as he walked down the corridor behind a kind looking lady dressed in a navy-blue cotton skirt and jacket, turning to smile reassuringly whilst holding the door open, she said 'please take a seat Mr Bailey' before following him into the small office.

A pair of robins chirped in the tree outside, causing the grieving widowers mind to wonder whether the old wives' tale was true, that the sight of a robin after someone's death is them trying to see you once more. Shaking his head and rubbing his eyes as he turned to

the Registrar.

'My name is Anne' she said in a soothing

voice - 'I'm responsible for registering deaths

in the Southampton area, I am really sorry for

your loss especially after such an unfortunate

accident.'

Jason looked sternly - 'it wasn't an accident,

they were murdered.'

'I'm sorry Mr Bailey, I can only go by the official verdict which was recorded as a road traffic accident' she said, sliding a piece of paper in front of him clearly stating such, Jase took one look at it - 'Lies, it's lies, they were murdered, the Police covered it up, this is utter nonsense.'

'Mr Bailey, I don't represent the Police, and I have no knowledge of the circumstances surrounding your family's death, all I can do is offer my condolences and help you finish the paperwork which will allow the burial of your loved ones as per your wishes, please allow me to help you get through this so you can find some sort of peace.' Jason, his head down, looked through the top of his eyes - a searing anger was boiling inside of him, but

he knew it wasn't Annes fault she was just a
pen pusher, another worker stuck in the
governments grip - 'I'm sorry for getting
angry, let's get this done.'

Reaching for the biro on her desk he signed
the paperwork for his beloved Sarah and
Milly, a tear in the corner of his eye dropped
on the sheet as he lifted his head backwards
- 'I need to go outside' he said anxiously 'no
problem, Mr Bailey, thank you for your time, I
will send the certificate to you as a matter of
urgency, god bless.'

Jason turned and walked through the corridor
and past reception before bursting into the
courtyard and kicking the wall in anger - 'I'm
gonna kill these vile reprobates' he growled,
'this comes from the top, it must be high level,

it's gotta be the Government, those savages
will pay.' Thumping the drainpipe, he exited
the carpark back onto Bugle Street.

Anger was burning through every sinew in his
body as he clenched an array of thick set
muscles honed by years in the gym and the
docks. After striding purposefully towards the
top of the street, Jason reached the Duke of
Wellington mumbling - 'now that's what I
need, a stiff drink and a few moments to
contemplate.'

In the bar a couple of people were playing
pool, with the rest of the room laying empty,
apart from the smiling barman - 'morning sir,
how can I help?'

'A large Scotch please fella and keep them
coming' Jason groaned 'here's to family,
friends and honour' he said raising a glass,

the barman nodded in approval as the new customer sank his second one.

Three hours later and more than slightly worse for wear Mr Bailey staggered into the street shielding his eyes from the bright sun, walking towards Bargate Street he aimed to catch the bus home but only made it a short way before landing in a crumpled heap on the pavement just short of Castle Street - in full view of a passing Police car.

'We've got a right one here' said PC Bryne turning the car round to scrape up the drunken sot. Standing over the dishevelled wreck the officer asked 'how many fingers am I holding up' - the more fingers he held up the more pairs Jason could see, unfortunately pairs are great if you're playing poker but not when convincing the law that you're sober.

Later that evening Jase woke to the sound of keys clanging on the cell door, his head was thumping, his mouth was like the bottom of a parrot's cage, and he stank of stale whisky - 'Wakey, Wakey Mr B, your little friend has come to rescue you, you're free to go.'

The prisoner rubbed his eyes, as if that would make any difference to his blurred vision. In the doorway an officer stood waving - indicating a need to move towards the open door, PC 77 held his nose - 'soup, soap and a shave is what you need, don't let me see you back here again.'

At reception his good mate Trev came into view - 'you silly sod, you had us all worried, come on mate let's get you home.'

Trev drove gently along the dual carriageway, partly because of his mate's thumping headache, partly because of the speed cameras but mainly due to potholes spanning the whole length of the road. Jason turned towards his kindly chauffeur - 'thanks Brother, I'm sorry to be a burden it's just that when the Registrar told me their deaths were the result of a road traffic accident, I lost it, the people who did this must wield a fair bit of power but they're still gonna suffer.'

'Absolutely mate, but for now let's get you back home, get you something to eat, showered and changed, before getting you tucked up in bed for the night, this kind of thing isn't going to help anyone, least of all you.'

Jason lightly punched Trev's arm - 'thanks buddy, I can always rely on you.'

The following morning, he woke in nice clean sheets, feeling a bit groggy but fresh, with the smell of bacon wafting up from the kitchen. Quickly throwing on something more suitable than underpants Jase ran downstairs expecting to see his darling Sarah rustling up some breakfast, unfortunately his dreams were shattered by the sight of Trev stood there in saggy boxers burning some bacon with his rotund belly hanging out.

'Morning mate, just rustling up some grub I think there's something wrong with the hob, it keeps burning stuff' he said laughing loudly - 'Bloody Hell Trev, I thought it was Sarah through the smoke' his mate laughed.

'Sorry mush I just figured you needed someone to look after you for a few days, till you get back on your feet.'

'Look after me? You call burning down my kitchen looking after me, come here you knob' Jason gave his mate a hearty slap on the back 'cheers Trev, I really appreciate this, but let's get down the caff and have something that won't kill us, oh and put some bloody clothes on - you ain't no pin up sunshine.'

A few days later the formalities of death were

concluded with the funeral arrangements

made. Jason and Sarah had pre-purchased a

burial plot but hadn't expected to be putting it

to use so soon.

It was a clear day in the Southampton

Cemetery, leaves rustled in the gentle breeze

as a group of mourners prepared to bid

farewell.

A tiny coffin lay next to its full-sized wicker neighbour both adorned with a beautiful array of flowers including a bouquet of Bluebells, Sarah's wildflower favourite.

A grief-stricken Jason solemnly walked across the damp grass and knelt to talk to his two precious souls - the river of love flowed deeply in their lives, and he couldn't imagine living without them, placing a single paper rose on Millie's casket sadness welled up in his eyes and anger in his heart as the full force of reality hit him in the chest like frenzied punches.

Fighting back tears and fury he returned to his clique of friends who looked equally strained by the emotions coursing through their minds.

Black freshly pressed suits alongside ladies'
bonnets and dark dresses gathered silently,
solemn with the loss of their friend and one so
young. Memories of Milly running around in
her pretty collection of clothes, playing on the
swings, and giggling with joy as she had fun
with her doting parents caused tears to flow
abundantly.

Looking towards the bereft father it was
difficult to watch a broken man who'd lost so
much in such strange circumstances, he
would find it easier if there were some straight
answers or someone to directly blame and
punish - but there was nothing, nobody to
direct their hatred and anger at apart from
some faceless charlatans in government, it

was going to take a long time to get over this, if indeed that was possible.

Woe betides the scum behind this deed, the congregation knew Jase wouldn't give up and his savagery would be launched against any perpetrator involved.

Jason stood silently by the graves clenching his fists until his knuckles were as white as a sheet, his parents, his wife, and his daughter were all dead, even though he was

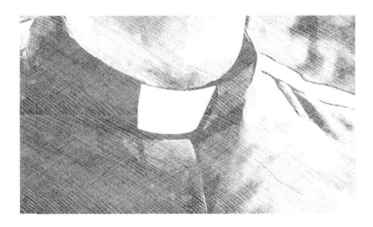

surrounded by people he still felt alone in the world, a complex mix of emotions caused him to shudder.

The Vicar stood in dark robes reading out a plethora of psalms before speaking warmly of Sarah and Milly describing the tragic loss, Jason's mind wandered remembering the happy times they'd spent together and the life they'd built, before a disturbing vision crept into his mind revealing Sarah's face as the life drained out of her, the guilt of it not being him and the feeling of hopelessness as he was unable to stop the bloodshed.

The voluble reverend eventually finished talking, indicating to Jason that he could say some words, politely declining and wiping a tear from his eye he sprinkled a handful of soil onto the coffins after they were gently lowered to rest. As he turned to walk away Trev kindly spoke - 'don't worry mate, we'll be here for you'.

Jase tried to raise a smile as they moved towards a nearby bench - 'I don't get it Trev; I still don't get it. The Police have done nothing, yet the van had a siren wailing, the men who jumped out had some form of military training, and they dragged five people into their vehicle. Nothing makes sense.'

Trev looked at his visibly shaken pal 'the truth will come out - I'm sure of it. You'll feel better when you come back to work next week'.

'They won't have me back Trev, not after getting well and truly caught pulling a sicky' Jason replied solemnly.

'I shouldn't worry about that mate, most of the hierarchy have gone missing since you've been off and we're proper short-staffed fella, Jimmy is fully in charge since the ghosting of our middle management structure - even the union don't know what's going on. The pencil pushers seem to have vanished, nothing's changed though, because we all know who does the real work and it certainly wasn't them with their agile working was it?'

Jason gazed into the distance, maybe it would be good to get back and take his mind off things. Nudging Trev, he stood up - 'we'd better get to the wake, you're a good friend

Trev, thanks for sticking by me.' After lighting a cigarette, the pair walked in silence passing through the sea of graves en-route to the waiting funeral cars.

Latterly, a gleaming black limousine pulled up outside the Ship Inn, the friends exited the vehicle - walking straight towards the pub, both minds were cinqued with idea of drowning their sorrows while leaning on the ancient oak bar and chatting with locals, most of whom were coworkers in the docks.

Another vehicle slowly drifted to the opposite curb; its windows tinted as if to hide the occupants. Through the open side window, a long camera lens could be seen snapping shots of Jasons friends before retreating into the shadowy cab.

Oblivious to the unwelcome visitors outside Jasons eyes fixated on the beckoning brass taps, licking his lips he strode up to the landlord - 'Hiya Dave, mines a lager please fella and Trev will have a Guinness.'

'I'm so sorry to hear about your family mate, it must have been a right harrowing time – these one's are on me mush' Dave proceeded to pull two inviting glasses of alcohol.

Jason looked up 'thanks mate, really appreciated. I'm still trying to get my head round the nightmare and it's absence from the news - it's all proper sinister mush, but I intend to find out what the hell is going on because the cruel filth who killed my family deserve to be in the ground, not them.'

'If there's anything I can do' Dave responded -
'please just ask, I know a few people and we
will be more than happy to help you out,
nobody gets away with this especially against
one of our own.'

Jason raised his glass before shouting across
the room

'Sarah and Milly, never forgotten and always in
our hearts.' A supportive cheer rang throughout
the pub as Jason took a massive slurp from his
pint before slamming it on the bar, 'don't worry
mate, we'll get the arseholes' said Trev putting
a supporting hand on his mate's shoulder - but
for now, we may as well get drunk, Dave, same
again please mush.'

Billy walked up to Jason - 'did you see that black crew cab outside mate, looked genuinely dodgy to me?'

They walked to the window - 'that one over there mate, it turned up at the same time as us, I swear it was at the cemetery.' Jason walked to the door, flung it open and ran towards the vehicle - almost immediately it spun its wheels and hurtled off in the direction of Nursling at an incredible rate of knots, he gave chase for a few seconds but realised it was worthless - 'Tossers' he shouted at the top of his voice 'I'll find out who you are, then you'll be sorry.' Turning to Billy he said, 'come on lad, let's get back inside and thanks for letting me know, sharp eyes son, sharp eyes.'

EPISODE 4 – Back to the Grind

Briskly flailing in the direction of a bedside cabinet Jason fumbled for the alarm, today was his first day back to work, a mix of emotions ran through his brain as he struggled to bring himself round, there was the pain from missing his family and the worry towards the reception he would receive at work - but overall, Jase was looking forward to seeing his mates, it would be a good distraction.

Staggering downstairs, he picked up one of Milly's toys, holding the fluffy pink elephant to his face a tear trickled from a sleepy, sad looking eye.

Pans and plates nestled in the sink whilst the fridge laid bare, widower Bailey made a cup of black coffee before muttering 'I wasn't hungry anyway.'

Sitting at the table he scanned the news, several headlines screamed about millions of missing people - after rapidly turning from sceptic to convert Jasons face contorted as he thumped the table angrily bouncing last night's plates into the air 'SCUM' he growled 'I knew there was something going on' with glaring eyes and a rapidly reddening neck he slammed the kitchen door, stormed upstairs, and threw his clothes on ready for work.

Forklifts drove busily around the docks, lights still blazed from the night shift and the bustle of stevedores filled the sea air.

A voice shouted - 'Welcome back mush, anything you need just shout mate' Trev said as he ushered his pal towards the canteen. A cheer erupted when they walked through the door, a wry smile crept across Jason's face, it felt good to be back.

Donning his grubby Hi-Viz jacket and white hardhat the memories of the past few weeks were gone for a moment.

The rain poured steadily throughout the morning as copious quantities of containers were manoeuvred onto waiting lorries and trains, a hive of activity that continued until the lunchtime claxon sounded allowing the soaking wet workers to amble towards the warmth of their rest areas.

Billy was huddled against the radiator as the remaining crew shuffled into the small brick building once used by dock security, now the favourite haunt of Trev's gang because it was away from the main canteen and a fair bit quieter, without people trying to talk over each other - but additionally bonused by being out of sight of previously clockwatching management stooges.

Nick scrolled through news stories on his phone before stopping abruptly at a breaking headline 'Over a Million Missing Across the UK' - he inquisitively read on 'Families from around the nation have reported neighbours disappearing overnight, some bundled into vans some vanishing inexplicably without a trace. The Police have refused to comment as reports come in their droves'... Looking startled he shouted to the rest of the guys to keep it down as he relayed the main parts of the story to them.

Jason looked on, listening intently, figuring the
cause of his families untimely death was a
chase across the city as another family tried
to escape in their 4x4 - his thoughts were
interrupted by Charlie shouting - 'who cares
mate, at least it weren't us' some of the other
guys nodded their heads in agreement as
Charles added 'there's a few managers gone
missing round here but to be fair they were all
tossers and nobody's missed them, maybe
it's for the best?'

Billy stood up, leaving the warm glow of the
radiator to state 'it may not be us now - but it
could be in future, remember the Martin
Niemöller poem from World War 2.

He began eloquently reciting –

'First, they came for the Communists, and I did not speak out because I was not a Communist.

Then they came for the Socialists, and I did not speak out because I was not a Socialist.

Then they came for the trade unionists, and I did not speak out because I was not a trade unionist.

Then they came for the Jews, and I did not speak out because I was not a Jew.

Then they came for me, and there was no one left to speak for me.'

Charlie blasted - 'Yeah and what's your point college boy?' to which Billy retorted 'don't sit on your laurels, it could be your family next, you selfish man.'

Billy had a thirst for politics whether it was Proudhon or Parliament, BBC, or mainstream media he analysed, dissected, and formulated opinions on the agendas of those in charge before sharing his ideas online, engaging with others in deep political thought between several shadow bans issued by every social media outlet, he wasn't about to allow Charlie to get away with shutting him down with abusive language. 'Education is a vital tool' he continued - 'we all need to analyse and question what we read especially when the info comes from the self-appointed voices of the people in the media, who are paid to regurgitate the opinions of our so-called democratic leaders.'

'Not another conspiracy theory' Charlie shouted - 'you really are an idiot Billy, shut the hell up and let the grownups speak' he bellowed tersely whilst making derogatory signs with his hands.

Billy stood up sharply - 'swearing and abuse
are the reactions of the inarticulate and ill-
educated' he boomed at Charles who looked
startled, the argument started to become
heated with differing opinions amongst the
whole group until Jason shouted - 'THEY
KILLED MY WHOLE FAMILY, what more

evidence do you bloody well need?' veins were popping in his neck and with clenched fists accompanied by the look on his face everyone knew it meant trouble.

The room immediately went quiet, you could've heard a pin drop. Jason composed himself before saying in a calm steady voice - 'calm down lads, Billy may be onto something there, a lot of strange things have been happening lately especially as they only seem to be targeting the management structure and those who believe themselves to be the middle classes, it may not be us at the moment but once they've finished with them it could be us next, we've got to stick together and work out what the hell is going on, now is not the time for infighting.'

Trev stepped forward and interjected - 'look you lot, it's not inconceivable that the shower in Westminster is up to something I know of at least ten families who've had relatives disappear overnight, their homes laying empty.

It's like they'd been kidnapped - ten whole families don't get kidnapped in one night - especially when they don't have £Millions in the bank. Keep an open mind.'

Wrapping up, he looked around the room - 'Billy could be right, everyone has something to lose, be it family, friendship, relationships, property, whatever makes you tick, but someday it could all be torn from you - like

Jason here, he's lost his family, his whole life has been torn apart and nobody knows why.'

Billy chipped in - 'call me a conspiracist but I think we all know what our elected representatives are capable of, and it ain't all good is it? I might be young, but I analyse things, I research, and I look deeper into stuff. Jasons correct, there is something peculiar, we are a crew, and crews are bonded, we need to look out for one another.'

Charlie shook his head - 'I can't see it, but hell guys we shouldn't be arguing like this, sorry Jase I can't imagine the pain you're going through and I'm sorry if I've been a bit insensitive mate.'

'Sensitive isn't something I'd associate with you … you stupid great lump' said Jason laughing as he fist-pumped his colleague 'come on mush, let's get back to grind before we get our pay docked.'

Donning his grimy hard hat, he strode purposefully through the canteens double fire doors, the stench of diesel fumes hitting him as the welcome sun struck his narrowed eyes with radiant beams finding their way between the miles of containers waiting patiently whilst rusting on the dock - behind the exterior calmness in his face Jasons head was buzzing.

He relived the pain after the occupants of the governments van leapt forth with two of them intercepting him as he launched himself

61

forward lashing violently to free himself and comfort his family. The pain of the Bazer tearing through his body as muscles tightened uncontrollably, before he was beaten unmercifully around his knees, falling to the floor convulsing, and crying out in agony.

The absconding family being dragged helplessly from their 4x4, fear expressed clearly across blood-soaked faces – a husband, wife and three children, cuffed, bruised, and battered being thrown into the waiting van.

The crowd who did precisely nothing to prevent the episode as the government agency vehicle screeched off the pavement, vanishing as quickly as it had arrived, his own electrocuted bruised and battered frame leaning on the jeep with his face wracked as he sobbed uncontrollably staring skywards after his whole life had been ripped apart before him, Sarah and Milly crushed to a pulp, staring lifelessly down the high street. 'I only wanted a day with my family and a frigging pie' he thought to himself.

At this point he imagined Billy trying to calm him down by quoting father of mindfulness, Buddhist zen master Nhất
Hạnh who said - 'anger is an energy that people use to act. But when you are angry, you are not lucid and may do wrong things. That is why compassion is a better energy.' Jason muttered to himself, 'that bell end can

do one, I'm gonna kill them all anyway.... end of.'

'What's that mate' said Trev, Jason's head snapped back, 'sorry mate' he retorted, turning to his pal 'I was just daydreaming - let's get back to work, those containers ain't gonna move themselves fella.'

The crew picked up the pace, their gate becoming more urgent - attempting to get back to their positions before anyone noticed any tardiness. It was odd that since the management had disappeared the workforce had pulled together, united in their endeavours working strongly as a team and to be fair becoming more productive as a result - it certainly seemed a happier place without the usual 'Seagull Management' who swooped in, made lots of noise, and pooped on everyone before flying off again.

EPISODE 5 – Collection Day

The early morning mist became threaded with
headlight beams as a sleepy suburb on the
outskirts of Winchester burst with activity, like
a sea of ants the legions of armour-clad foot
soldiers poured relentlessly from idling
vehicles before donning gas masks and firing
gas canisters randomly through beckoning
windows.

Reminiscent of black uniformed fascist thugs
of the past they battered down doors with
huge steel rams before dragging limp
occupants from their homes, overcome by the

noxious air there was no resistance as bodies were loaded into the waiting motorcade.

'Don't smash them about and squash them too much' an aggressive authoritarian voice howled, 'they need them alive for processing and harvesting, they're no good dead because the corpse begins to rot'.

As quickly as it had arrived the vehicular convoy sped away leaving empty houses behind.

A dog lay silent on the blood-soaked rug, a single bullet administered to its skull to prevent a plague of strays when the anaesthetic gas wore off. Distorted sounds from some tacky tv game show failed to compete with the blistering sound of Slipknot pumping through the eldest son's bedroom floor.

Moments ago, this was a family home, now it had the hallmarks of a warzone, but without a single human casualty in sight, they'd disappeared into the night with their government assassins as the macabre body heist continued.

Driving north on the M3 a man sat shaking in one of a fleet of collection vehicles 'you ok mate?' the driver asked,
'guess this was your first night.'

The passenger looked up 'yeah, I didn't really expect this' - his whitened face grimacing as he thought about those they'd dragged from their homes, 'don't worry mate it gets easier

the more runs you do - my names John
what's yours.'

'Brian…' said the new boy, trying to compose
himself.

As the Winchester Services exit came into
view Brian asked, 'why are we indicating,
they're shut look at the signs' - John laughed
'we've got full run of the place tonight, this is
where we drop off our load and go out for
more - after having something to eat
obviously, I'm starving' Brian immediately
responded - 'I don't think I could face
anything to be fair.'

Tower lights lit the carpark like it was daytime,
bodies were being taken from the waiting
vans, loaded into a racking system to keep

them upright, then firmly strapped in before being sent to processing centres around the country. Brian stared in disbelief - 'there must be over 150 lorries here constantly collecting payloads from endless streams of vans, this is way bigger than I imagined.'

John looked at him straight faced - 'it's all necessary son, we're overpopulated, all we are doing is thinning the herd, just make sure you don't let anyone know you have doubts, or you'll become a victim too.'

Brian sat quietly for the rest of the night, the silent assembly had made the conscious decision to stay shtum, it seemed much easier and visibly more sensible to look after number one than get involved - the pay wasn't bad either.

EPISODE 6 – Parliamentary Decisions

The following day there were no clouds in the
sky, as traffic meandered through London's
streets at a crawl, frustratingly getting stuck at
one set of red lights before being released to
stop at the next - people sat outside coffee
bars sipping the latest multi-titled hot drink as
others frantically scurried along the
pavements late for work again.

Adjacent to Parliament a small crowd had
gathered protesting the lack of action towards
these unusual disappearances. John, a tall
scruffy man clad in jeans and leather was
holding a sign emblazoned with the words -
'it'd be better if Parliament disappeared.' He

stood proudly amongst three other brave

souls determined to make their point.

Lisa was just out of university and had turned

up with her best friend Mandy, then there was

Pete, he was a veteran campaigner anything

he could get involved in he would - from

shouting down unelected world bodies foisting ideologies on the global population, to protesting proxy wars Pete had always made every effort to protest.

In recent years College Green became somewhat silent, mass demonstrations had previously been quashed after heavy handed private contractors were employed to remove dissenting mobs, or individuals.

The last major protest involved a crowd of 10,000 angry activists fighting the imposition of Photo/DNA identification on every single member of society - controlling the population, restricting civil liberties, and treating citizens like criminals was viewed as a step too far – ironically, actual criminals wouldn't be affected as they'd undoubtedly forge their own identification and create new markets selling to others.

On that fateful day a huge contingent of military uniformed contractors had been drafted in, all clad in body armour, donning Bazers, firearms and tear gas.

With the appearance of a Darth Vader collective on steroids they were a formidable sight for protesters amassed on the green and surrounding streets.

Tension rose in the air; loud chants rang rhythmically in time with four drummers stood tauntingly at the front of a baying crowd. Without warning the leader of the government's forces shouted 'ENGAGE' - within seconds stun grenades blasted on the green, tear gas engulfed the air and a brutal militia piled into the startled mob.

There was stiff resistance at first with protesters smashing placards over the heads of their attackers, punching relentlessly to hold them back and kicking anything dressed in a uniform.

The line stayed strong until the militia started to shoot live rounds amongst the throng, blood spewed into the air, screams filled the green - some through the pain of being shot, some through abject fear. This wasn't the way a peaceful protest had been met in the past; everyone ran for their lives.

A man nestled on the floor next to his dying partner, he gently ran his fingers through her hair before falling forward after being shot by a marauding contractor enjoying himself far too much, whilst continuing to fire at random targets as if part of a demonic turkey shoot.

The aftermath was a mess, forty-three people died that day, in the following weeks a government enquiry was released to the media claiming that - 'members of the unruly degenerates had opened fire on the peace keeping forces resulting in a small and controlled retaliation to restore order.' Everyone knew it was a cover up, but no one had the guts to step forward and say it, especially in Parliament as they feared for their jobs and their £140,000 salary (plus expenses). The whole saga had drifted silently from the public's memory.

Pete remembered that day all too well, he had
lost a good friend, a comrade from many
campaigns was mown down by the dispersing
crowd, receiving head injuries so severe he
died within days of the event. Today's vigil
was tiny, and he honestly believed the
government wouldn't react in such a way, this
wasn't a third world dictatorship after all.

Unfortunately, he couldn't be more wrong, a
blacked-out medium sized panel van glided
briskly round the corner its side door open in
readiness, approaching the four shocked
protesters a group of militia leapt onto the
green, Bazed the quintet and threw them into
the van - within moments the vehicle
disappeared.

Pete lay on the vans load bed, a foot pressed heavily on his chest whilst his hands and feet were cuffed, memories of his friend came flooding back as the current predicament became all too clear. 'You lot are in for it now' shouted one of the masked mercenaries - growling directly into Lisa's face he grunted menacingly 'you will never cause any trouble again, because today, my little lady you will be going to our processing centre, from whence there's no return.'

Lisa's lip quivered as she lifted her shoulder to wipe spit from her face after the guard's saliva spraying rant - 'you utter bastard' she squealed before receiving a size ten boot in her face and passing out on the cold corrugated floor with a loud thump, bruising

slowly ruining her pretty features and blood

discolouring strands of long blonde hair, their

future was as bleak as a drove of pigs

entering an abattoir.

Meanwhile, inside Parliament, insulated from

society a pathetically small group of MPs

discussed current events. Ricky, a blonde

man of the north spoke openly - 'we voted for

the cull, we knew what we were doing, and

we knew the consequences of it, our nation is

grossly overpopulated, and radical action was

required. We are here to represent the interests of Great Britain which is what we did. The UK requires a cull, those taken for processing should be proud to be given the opportunity to help their fellow man, someone had to make the decision, and they should be grateful that we rose to the occasion.'

Mavis an MP from the Shires retorted - 'but Ricky, I don't believe we all knew what depths it would go to.'

'Depths??' Ricky responded - 'we knew what depths, we knew the population would be culled, we chose the Middle Classes as victims because their jobs can easily be passed to the workers without renumeration, we only ever had middle management to provide well paid salaries to a few of our voters and keep ourselves elected, you of all people should recognise that fact, your businesses are flourishing without the detritus in the middle - they are surplus to requirement and the herd needed thinning.'

Mavis sat silent; she'd felt a bit guilty before, but less so now as she'd put her objection forward and could rightfully post on social media to proudly claim 'I tried'.

Timothy, one of the Eton cohort was next to speak 'we are all complicit in this decision, a decision as Ricky rightly stated was taken in the interests of our nation. Those who are worried that the citizens of the UK will avoid us at the next General Election only need to look at the previous hundred years to recognise these lemmings will only ever vote for Red or Blue, they are easily led, in fact stupid to the degree that they forget so easily the misdemeanours of our past, the mistakes we've made and the £Billions it's cost them as taxpayers - come on everybody you cannot tell me that killing a few of these miserable oiks is going to make a blind bit of difference, especially when we've taken over the homes of those we've culled, and made them available as Social Housing.

These morons will forgive and forget once they've been rewarded with a bit of luxury and ended their wealth envy, of course that's if they can afford the rent.' he scoffed loudly as the subservient house laughed with him.

From the shadows a deep voice boomed 'when a government is as transparent as mud

there's always going to be accusations of
corruption slithering through the halls of
power and staining the walls of democracy,
however the trick is to distract them with a
seemingly more important crisis to draw their
focus'.

Bill Blackburn strode forward and continued -
'the public have been conditioned over
centuries; these servile creatures have
neither the bravery nor the brains to fight
back. A path untrodden is a missed
opportunity, equally a vote given without
explorative efforts is a waste of paper, but
these utter prats keep doing the same thing,
time and time and time again.

British voters can be likened to a shoal of fish
watching the nasty shark pull the plug out of

their pool - knowing the consequences, they still do nothing in the hope that the mad shark will eventually put the plug back in and everything will return to normal.'

Stroking his chin, he said thoughtfully - 'voting the same way or doing the same thing whilst expecting a different result is like cleaning your teeth with sugar to avoid tooth decay -

these people are dead sheep, if we fail to respond to the pathetic chirping of our constituents not one of them comes back for another go, merely accepting there's no point.

The UK has disruptors and apologists in equal measure, the trick is to get them to fight each other - division is the new world order my friends, never forget that!!

Reading through social media they both seem to use made up words like Moronalistic, Pratmodical, Charlatinical or Arsefacery in a vain attempt to gain likes and followers to plump their ego's on social media, I doubt these ingrates have the backbone or ability to mount any kind of attack upon us and they certainly won't unite against Parliament, because they're too self-interested.'

As Bill sat down with a smug look on his saggy jowelled face, Roland - one of the newer members of the house piped up - 'Bill' he said hesitantly 'aren't you afraid of losing your seat at the next General Election......?' a huge deep laugh filled the room.

'Afraid.... afraid, Ho, Ho, Ho.... Don't be daft sonny, even if I do lose my seat, I will make £Millions in the city or with the companies I own, then I'll get back in power at the next time round boosted by election funding from my newfound sponsors after taking a rather nice five-year sabbatical - career politicians don't suffer we evolve.'

Roland looked sheepish it wasn't the answer he was expecting. 'Dear boy' Bill bellowed, 'you have a lot to learn if you're going to make it in politics, I suggest you take a leaf out of the Labour and Tory grandees who've never really put forward an objection and managed to replicate their stance for the past century, nothing has changed with their collective approach, and nothing ever will change in Parliament - because the public are scared of change, and we all know it.

The house fell into disrepute many years before even I came along, discipline was a word one would never associate with it - even the Speaker has lost power over our unruly mob. I don't care if the public believe us to be self-interested charlatans, them morons will keep voting for us because they are conditioned puppets created over a very long period, a social experiment that we lead – you will have to make your mind up which side you are on, and quickly.'

Bill finished and stared at Roland, a raised eyebrow and side on menacing look was enough for the inexperienced pup to reply - 'sorry sir, no offence intended, I certainly know which side I am on, would you like me to buy you a drink?'

Bill leapt to his feet, as quickly as an overweight establishment lump could - 'Right Mr Speaker mines a large whisky, let's take the rest of the day off' he concluded. A pathetic parade of MP's followed his word, acting like the sheep they accuse the electorate of being.

After a rousing hip, hip hooray Parliamentary business fell silent for the day as the Speaker looked solemnly on.

Meanwhile in Prime Minister (PM) Grants office Tilinda Desouza, the environment minister stood before her PM, who was grinning lustfully behind his desk. She had a good figure for someone in their late 40's - after starting her career as an athlete, winning three golds at three consecutive Olympics, her delft like figure hadn't gone unnoticed to several male politicos who couldn't keep their eyes off her.

The PM was doing one of his usual self-appreciation speeches, puffing and preening himself as he spewed out a stream of disgraceful admissions to an audience with as much resistance as the dead.

This time he was explaining how control works - 'firstly you have to create and present a crisis, or a target of hate to the majority of the population, you know - like when I allowed people to walk slowly in the road to make a political point, it disrupted everyone's lives, stopped them getting to work, taking kids to school, getting friends and family to hospital, and doing their daily routines. After my agents had pushed the agenda on social media, I told the police to do nothing, to engage peacefully with the protest, give them refreshments and arrest any member of the public who tried to interfere or forcibly remove protesters blocking the road.

I created a monster, a demon a focus of hate
and consolidated anger throughout the nation
– resulting in British citizens supporting the
reduction of their own civil liberties to see
these apparent demons punished.

Like a guardian angel floating down to save these earthly forms I introduced the most draconian, restrictive, antidemocratic, anti-demonstration bill possible, whilst Britons across our nation applauded profusely.

They had fallen for my psychological trick, happily signed away their right to strike, demonstrate or even argue against their imperial master.'

It may have been the sunlight, but as Grant finished pontificating his eyes almost seemed to glow, he had a demonic tone in his cackling laughter whilst swinging to and frow in the creaking tan leather chair.

The Minister stood before him stunned but in pretend awe of her master - 'Oh Prime

Minister you will certainly be remembered as the man who shaped our society - controlling the public has always been like trying to herd cats but you seem to have a natural flare for it, well done sir, very well done' she gushed grovelingly hoping to get a wage rise, unaware the only rise she would be offered laid in PM Grants underpants.

'Now that's enough about me, let's talk about you' he simpered lecherously whilst rubbing his crotch. 'Thank you, Prime Minister, I have come to talk about the green targets we set last year' Tilinda replied questioningly.

'Tilly love, you don't need to keep calling me Prime Minister, PM will suffice – anyway, my utter, utter brilliance has led to our green targets being achieved much quicker than programmed. It's all to do with Body Fuel, he said swinging in the giant revolving leather chair, all he needed was a cat in his lap and this revolting man would cut the figure of the perfect Bond Villain. 'It's like this' he continued, 'my idea to cull the miserable wretches identifying as middle class, has led to a completely new eco-fuel.

From the bloated beasts crushed cadavers we've been able to extract fat and oil, then after some incredibly special scientific processes, Hay Ho – here's loads of free fuel to produce blended eco formulas, plenty of pocket money for yours truly and a bloody nice splash of greenwashing for good measure. Man, I'm good, you can see why they keep voting me in as PM, can't you ....' he said expectantly.

Cowering in front of the desk, the timid looking Environment minister started nodding profusely to please her overbearing boss. 'Yes sir, you really are special' she said crawlingly like a frightened mouse.

'I surprise myself sometimes darling' he replied, licking his lips as he looked her up and down observing every curve of her beautiful form, before glancing over to see the photograph of his wife staring him down menacingly.

Placing the photo frame on its front as if to hide the gaze and relieve his conscience the dirty old letch leant forward attempting to capture his sexual prey, before the door burst open and in bounced Blackburn.

'PUB?' Bill boomed as he leered at Tilinda - 'cold shower, then pub you filthy old sod, come on you lustful gigolo this one will wait till later and Rowland will put all the booze on his expenses - sorry Tilly baby, Tarzan here has other business to attend to' he shouted laughingly whilst Grant stood rubbing his privates in her general direction.

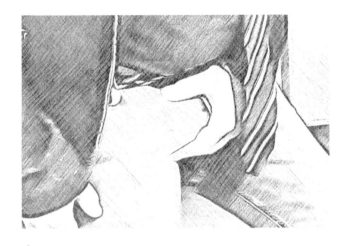

OK, Bill – I will get back to my environmental drilling programme later' cackled the PM as the two Etonians roared with laughter.

Desouza made a quick exit too, running down the corridor as fast as an ex - Team GB athlete in stiletto heels could manage, 'that was a lucky escape, good grief I would've probably puked with that repugnant lump writhing all over me' she said to herself

shivering at the mere thought of it - before

locking her office door, downing three cans of

gin and tonic from the fridge next to her desk

and collapsing on the couch, it was going to

be a long five year Parliamentary term for this

fine filly.

EPISODE 7 – The Processing

Bursting forth from the clouds a sleek grey

helicopter flew across the Kent countryside,

its occupants in deep discussion. Prime

Minister Grant - a smug looking man revered

by many, hated by more, was nursing a

hangover after piling as much alcohol onto

Rolands's expenses account as he possibly

could, the pompous PM slouched in his seat

puffing on a fat cigar as his assistant stared at the no smoking sign, failing to muster the courage to say anything.

Putting the newspaper down the PM started to speak 'you know what' he said gruffly 'Britain doesn't know how lucky it is to have me, running a nation requires radical solutions and all the public can do is grizzle about a few thousand useless people being removed from society for the greater good'.

Bob turned towards his boss 'you're doing a marvellous job' he snivelled - 'the population reduction measures are surging rapidly towards our target, and we will hit 100,000 a day once our northern plants start up next week.'

A huge factory loomed in the distance, in complete contrast to the surrounding countryside.

As Grant's helicopter landed noisily in the car park, a group of Hi Viz clad workers in suits stood patiently on the tarmac to greet their illustrious leader.

'Welcome Prime Minister' the plant manager beamed, thrusting his arm forth to shake hands, 'you're going to love what we've done here; production is ramping up, security is impregnable with two hundred members of an elite armed force surrounding the area and we are processing the subjects 186% quicker than last week.

The PM responded, 'Good to meet you Dave, I've heard a lot about you - I'm looking forward to seeing this facility, lead the way let's have a look round.'

The group walked up a row of freshly created concrete steps and after passing through a large, galvanised steel door the enormity of the plant became clear, with conveyer belts full of bodies working tirelessly to move the 'merchandise' through the recycling process.

Contorted and bloodied bodies bumped mercilessly along its rubber belt. Faces stared out, ghostlike, unable to move or comment, although their eyes spoke a thousand words.

Pete lay amongst the hoard, he could clearly

see the Prime Minister, his mind raged but he couldn't move, every victim was drugged to sedate them, so they were awake but paralysed.

A woman described the crushing process as 'working far better when the cadavers are relaxed, 'we use a mixture of flunitrazepam and blood thinners to put our guests into a semi-conscious state, that way their bodily ingredients are much easier to extract - of course they know what's going on, but the fear will only last for a matter of minutes - it's perfectly acceptable and has been signed off by the Health Minister.'

Pete stared at the PM wishing him dead, wishing that the public had listened to him and his comrades, moreover, wishing the pair

CITIZEN PIES

Packed with British ingredients

going to be the last thing he saw, but this wasn't a movie where he'd make some incredible escape before taking down the villain, this was his last moments, this was the result of an out-of-control government, this was going to be excruciating but he couldn't even scream.

As Pete began to disappear through the rollers, Dave turned to the PM - 'bodies start off here where they are pierced and lightly crushed to extract the blood and fluids.

Moving along the conveyor he continued 'this unit is a boiling bath to loosen the meat from the bones, the good meat will go into our range of pies – Citizen Pies was such a great idea PM, and the public seem to love them, apparently it's better than lab grown meat and

106

tastes like chicken - although I guess if they knew it's true origin, they'd hold a different view.

We had a real bonus last week sir, 25kg of cocaine was found inside some very naughty drug mules - one of my guys is loading it onto your helicopter as we speak.'

The Prime Minister nodded approvingly.

Dave continued - 'The next phase is where we strip the remaining muscle, skin, and sinew from the carcass before finally collecting the gold teeth, titanium knees and other precious metals.

We've been able to reduce our carbon footprint by using body fat to fuel the generators, humans are also composed from

a high percentage of water - so we filter it,
and use the liquid as part of our clean down
activities - absolutely nothing goes to waste,
even the blood, brains and bone are being
used for fertiliser or vitamin tablets, skin and
leftovers go into pig feed whilst their clothing
is recycled by breaking the materials into
fibres, putting them through a fluffing process
and creating a new form of insulation for the
construction industry, similar to rockwool.

Moving swiftly on Dave continued to gloat 'we
have increased our pig farm ten-fold since the
start and will be exporting excess pork for
profit. This plant is utilising every technical
advance possible, and we are learning a
great deal too - it's just a shame we will have
to shut down at some point.'

'That's what you think' the Prime Minister mumbled.'

'Sorry I missed that' said Dave

'There's not much of a stink' the PM quickly responded.

Dave explained 'that's down to the seven-stage air filtration system we've installed - you could build one of these units in the suburbs and nobody would know, it's quiet, utilises robotics to keep staff to a minimum and doesn't exhaust any pollution into the environment.'

Grant looked pleased as punch, his mind was buzzing - 'through this process' he thought to himself 'we will be able to remove all burdens on society, be they old age pensioners,

criminals, the homeless, everyone on
benefits, hospital bed blockers, absolutely
anyone whose disabled or mentally ill, all
political agitators who disagree with the
greater good and especially the hordes of
migrant scum – legal or otherwise, who've
come here to live it up courtesy of state
handouts.'

Forgetting where he was for a moment, huge
lines formed across his face as an
uncontrollable belly-laugh burst out, echoing
through the full length of the factory unit.
Turning confidently towards his shocked
entourage Grant quickly composed himself
and recovered the moment by expressing his
gratitude to the 'kind hosts who'd been good

enough to give up their valuable time to show him round.'

The PM's face was still beaming as he climbed aboard the helicopter, his plan was in motion, anyone who didn't agree with him could be disposed of in one of these facilities and his share prices were rocketing after removing layers of unrequired management, the future was bright for those in power.

'Oh, I am good, world leaders eat your hearts out' he muttered to himself before sniggering quietly and adjusting the seat belt round his expanding girth.

The helicopter flew into the distance as quickly as it had arrived.

Dave walked back inside smiling contently to himself, 'after years of hard work I've finally made it' he thought to himself.

Entering the building he surveyed his little empire like a new-born king entering his castle, believing he was invincible, a person of power, someone who was relied on and would rightly be rewarded – ignorantly failing to recognise he was a wretched pawn utilised for 'uncomfortable' deeds, ready to take the fall and protect his unimpeachable masters.

Over millennia an unimaginable number of the ruling class fraternity had stood in front of Judicial Hearings claiming to know nothing, whilst accusing their advisors of being useless communicators, claiming colleagues had gone rogue, or their chamber had been infiltrated by foreign spies, before having

them all sacked and imprisoned - Dave's life

was only valuable while he was useful.

EPISODE 8 – The Shed

It had been a long day; Jason was finding it tough back at work, but it had provided a welcome distraction for the past three weeks. Sprawled on the settee his TV played the usual repeats accompanied with puerile adverts selling things you didn't know you needed, until they told you that you did.

A tray lay on the floor with evidence of another takeaway, this time his stomach had been victim to a Chicken Vindaloo, six poppadom's, three cans of lager and a half-opened pack of chocolate biscuits, he was still coming to terms with single life - replacing the gym with fast food may not have been the best thing but sometimes comfort food is

good for the mind - well that's what he told

himself.

A bright moon shimmered through whispery clouds glistening against the windowpane.

Outside a shuffling of feet could be heard - Jason dragged himself from his slumber and stared into the darkness, someone was in his shed.

Bursting through the back door he ran towards the outbuilding before rugby tackling a gym-toned Spaniard trying to make his escape. The duo wrestled for a while before Jason managed to get the intruder in a firm lock hold.

'What the hell do you think you're doing' he shouted angrily 'Lo siento, I'm sorry por favor don't call the autoridades' the man whimpered 'they've asesinatos, they've killed my familia, my whole familia….and they will assassinate me……I have nada, nowhere to stay' he pleaded, before falling to the floor gasping for breath as the powerful grip was released.

'Come on' said Jason 'let's go inside.'

Walking towards the house they turned to look at each other 'it seems we have something in common' Jase said enquiringly 'let's go in the kitchen and get you cleaned up.'

The kettle boiled in the background as Dominguez relayed his story with tears rolling down each cheek of a clearly distressed face.

'Last night's I'm getting in from work, my Sofia

was making dinner in kitchen she looked

stunning in her spray on jeans, perfect

breasts...' Jason interrupted, 'the basics

mate, stick to the basics.'

'Sorry campanero, I get carried away. My

wife, she makes la comida, the dinner we

sitting down with our dos children - Lucia and

Ana, it's a lovely start to the evening. The girls
stay downstairs whilst I upstairs for the bath,
before I can undress there's a masivo noise,
breaking vaso, wood snapping and a loud
bangings – stun grenades, I think.

I holding the ears when a group of gobierno,
the government henchmen stormed the home
– they kicking and beat me before I jumping
out the window, landing in hedge
unconscious.

When I get back in house I smell toxic gas in
air - I find blood poolings in the kitchen where
familia had fallen to floor cracking the heads
on ceramic tiles - they'd taken my esposa and
childrens bodies away whilst I was blacked
out, not having knowledge I was there - I
should have been able to proteger them, to

protect that's my elservicio, my duty, but I am failure.'

Tears swelling in his eyes he placed the only precious item he had left in the world on the table, a small photo of Sophia, Lucia, and Ana grinning at the lens. Jason stared at their smiling faces, flashbacks of his own tragic loss flooded through his mind 'don't worry Dom, there's nothing you could have done, I'll keep you safe - to be honest mate it looks like you and me need to get our revenge, these psychopaths have taken everything from both of us and believe me, they're gonna pay.'

Standing up Dom took Jason's hand, shaking it firmly he cleared his throat 'great to meeting you Jase, we get to it no? we sort these mothers out, will not sit by and let this regime brutalise familia across Britain, when do we start?'

'Soon my friend. very soon, you can lay low here whilst I sort a few things out - stay away from the windows, do not go out, do not turn the TV on when I'm out, do not contact anyone and most of all be patient, we will get these miscreants, you have my word. Now, I have some vindaloo left - do you fancy some?'

Dom looked at him, 'err, not for me - I'll pass gracias. I go baño, the toilet yes?'

'Go ahead mate, top of the stairs on the left, keep your voice down these walls have ears.'

Jason slumped into his favourite chair, the stuffing had gone and there was a fair bit of give in the cushions which made it lovely to snuggle into - flicking the TV on he started watching a news bulletin.

A studio presenter sat behind his desk beaming like he was in front of a modelling agency instead of delivering a news show, 'Welcome back from the break, our team have been looking into the current spate of disappearances across the UK and Cindy will take you through our findings.'

The screen switched from the studio to an outside broadcast where Cindy was stood before a huge factory complex surrounded by a high wall topped with razor wire, 'thanks Maurice - yes, we are outside a new factory that sprang up over the past few months, there's a hive of activity with several vehicles entering the site every hour of the day, the

security presence is like nothing I've ever

seen for an industrial unit. We have

interviewed residents who say they know

nothing of what's happening inside - in fact

the majority seem scared to even talk about

the current goings on.

We have contacted the occupants, but

they've refused to comment, quoting national

security or privacy laws - to be honest

Maurice it's all a bit sinister.'

He responded, 'what do the locals believe is

going on?'

'Well Maurice, as I said they've all been a bit

shy in coming forward but seem to believe it's

some sort of fertiliser factory or food

processing plant, nobody seems quite sure,

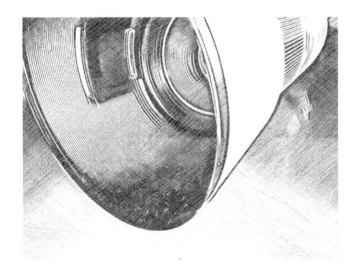

we have been in contact with the council, and

they refused to discuss it with us whilst

Companies House have no records of this

place.'

Cindy stopped abruptly, 'there seems to be some movement by the main gate Maurice, a group of armed soldiers are heading our way maybe they will have some answers for our viewers.'

The camera panned round to reveal the group of six adult males clad in military assault costume running towards them, almost immediately Cindy could be heard screaming as she was Bazed before being beaten round the side of the head and knocked out cold, the cameras' view shot up and sidewards as the operator fell to the floor after being shot in the leg and kicked in the head. The film kept rolling as the bloodied cameraman stared into the screen, his face screwed up with agony until a boot crushed the recording device and the screen went blank.

Back in the studio Maurice sat shaking in his chair staring in utter disbelief at what he'd just witnessed - hardly able to speak and looking ashen faced he meekly said 'let's take an ad break' before disappearing from the screen.

As the advertisements were running the set crew began talking angrily about the events, calling for someone to get down there and make sure their colleagues were OK.

From across the room someone shouted 'YES …. what an opportunity …. this has Pulitzer written all over it' - he went to grab his keys and equipment, but before he'd even got his hand out of his pocket he felt a sharp pain in his nose as the sound man punched him full in the face 'you degenerate arsehole, you're team-mates may be dead you sick mother, be grateful I don't kill you right now.'

From nowhere the studio lights went off - in the pitch-black screams rang out 'CALM DOWN' shouted Roger the sound man 'it's probably only tripped; I'll go and flick the fuses back on'.

Shuffling down the corridor he thought he could see a shadow but thought to himself it's just the darkness playing tricks on him - moving his hands along the wall he could feel a door frame 'ah that's the cutting room, next door on the left' he muttered to himself trying to stay calm. Further up the corridor seven shapes slipped quietly through the darkness,

127

their night vision goggles providing a perfect view of the intrepid hero. The hallway filled with light as Roger was Bazed and left convulsing on the floor.

'All clear Team Leader' came the voice over a radio, 'we're going in.'

Moving briskly down the corridor they could hear people in the studio, shots rang out as the assault continued inside - with bullets fired into people's knees to disable them, before being receiving a knockout blow to the skull.

The carnage occurred swiftly and efficiently, the leader looked rather pleased with himself - 'right lads, let's get the area cleaned up and put this lot in the wagon ready to be processed.'

Back in Southampton Jason was aghast at what he'd witnessed, the channel had stopped broadcasting and there was a banner across the TV stating 'Currently Off Air.'

Taking to social media there were thousands of posts appearing and disappearing in equal measure. 'What the bloody hell is going on' he grunted angrily 'these tyrants are out of control, someone's gotta stop this.'

He picked up his phone to call his mate, 'Trev, WHAT THE HELL - did you just see that on the news channel, Jesus mate I told you something was going on this is unbelievable.'

Jason introduced Dom and the trio chatted, comparing options, and debating what was going to happen next - it was early morning before they decided it was about time they went to bed, and to be honest Jase and Trev could finish their discussion at work in the morning - and earn some money whilst they did.

EPISODE 9 – The Plan

The following morning Jason got up for work,
stretching and arching his back he dropped to
the floor and started doing his press ups - 150
was his usual although the past few weeks
had taken their toll and today, he would likely
drop out at seventy.

Downstairs the kitchen looked like a bomb
had hit it, housework wasn't exactly his forte
and to be fair he really hadn't been in the
mood lately. After rustling up the obligatory
bacon sarnie to couple with his daughters
Honey Nuggets he walked into the lounge
and flopped in his chair. Dom was still asleep

on the couch, snoring lightly and muttering

the odd bit of Spanish, his mind was

obviously still on his loss.

Finishing his breakfast, he tapped Dom gently

on his shoulder, jumping as if to defend

himself the sleepy guest woke abruptly -

'morning' he said in a gravelled voice,

'what time is it?'

Jason looked on the mantle clock, his

wedding gift from the lads at work was just

about to strike five 'it's time I was off, nearly

five AM mate, you stay here

and keep away from the windows, my

neighbours know I'm at work and mid terrace

houses aren't built for privacy. I've left you

some food in the fridge, help yourself and I

will be back this evening, keep your head
down and I'll see you as soon as I can.'

Arriving through the gate Jason and his pals
were already discussing the previous night's
events, the whole yard was buzzing with
people showing each other's phones as if any
proof was required for the lack of stream on
social media, it's like it never happened.

Various posts were still up - however these
ones only stated that the whole thing was
from a movie company filming their latest
flick, or it was just a group of hoaxers having
a laugh at your expense. The odd thing was
that all the denial posts had the ability to
comment removed and any post which went
against the official narrative was immediately
deleted along with the accounts of those who

wrote it, liked it, or shared it.

On one social media outlet a trade union official started live-streaming – 'If we all become a pouting bottom lip republic devoid of any resistance other than moaning into the froth on our beer's humanity is lost and we may as well be amoeba aimlessly floating in the waters of life.

We must unite, we must resist, we must fight.......' The feed stopped abruptly, governmental control was swift, unrelenting, and efficient.

Surviving another long shift at the docks Jason was glad to get back home after the day's relentless discussions, Dom had been busy in the kitchen and his tea was on the table, a welcome sight to a half starved docker. 'Cheers fella, much appreciated, you'd make someone a good wife, a sodding ugly one, but at least one that can cook' he said laughing whilst taking a seat at the table.

'We are going out after we've had tea - you, me and the lads are gonna meet to discuss what we're going to do about the bastards who've killed our families, I'm guessing you're in?'

'Absolutely amigo, absolutely, we owe our familia, our niños and our mujeres.'

'All right Manuel, English please mate.' Said a baffled Jason.

'Our families, our children our women, we do it for them.'

Raising a bottle of beer, they clinked them together in approval before tucking into their piping hot dinner.

Subsequently, Jason strode down the hallway, unlocked the door and stepped into the garage revealing his beloved Betsi to a stunned Dominguez.

'Jesus Jase, guapisma, hermoso - she beautiful' he said standing in awe of the bright yellow Mk1 Ford Escort Mexico sat in front of him, with its number plate BET51 it wasn't hard to see why he'd picked the name.

Jason smiled as he stated 'she's running a two litre Pinto engine with 210 brake, twin Webbers, lightened flywheel, six-speed box with competition clutch, and an exhaust pipe that most drainage engineers would be proud of. She sits on sports suspension, has titanium arms all round with uprated brakes, vented discs complimented by and a lovely set of alloys. The list is endless, I've spent a load of time and money on her, she goes like a bullet and will pass everything apart from a fuel station.'

'I'm loving the colour' Dominguez replied, stroking the extra wide arches ballooning out from the gleaming bodywork - this really was a stunning full spec car.

Opening the door excitedly he slid into the passenger seat his body gripped by the buckets, holding him firmly in place. Looking round he admired the workmanship that had gone into building such a special vehicle -

from its shiny chrome roll bar to the custom aluminium dash she sure was an inviting ride.

Jason opened the boot, 'sorry mate you'll have to hide in here - being a fugitive and all that.'

His companion had disappointment written all over his face as he released himself from the safety harness and exited the car - 'Ok amigo, I'm understanding but por favor, take it easy, yes - it's not made for the comfortable riding in there.

'Looking over and smiling Jason jokingly retorted 'don't worry fella I'll keep her under a ton' sniggering to himself as he shut the boot 'come on Betsi, let's go for a run.'

Approaching his destination Betsi emitted a deep burbling sound - Jason smiled as he saw a couple of his pals come into view, rolling down his window he shouted 'Oi, Oi you lot, how's it going?'

Exiting his gleaming Ford, he walked over to his mates, 'well, well…fancy meeting you here, all a bit cloak and dagger ain't it.' he said laughing 'I have someone I'd like you to meet, his names Dom, he's had the same problem as me and wants to give us a hand.'

'Hold on mucker' said Finn, 'how do we know he's not one of them, why should we trust him?'

'Because my friend' Jason replied, 'his family has been wiped out, he's been beaten nearly half to death and he came to me for help, we need all the muscle we can get - now let me open the boot and get him out before the poor sod suffocates.'

Rubbing his eyes and stretching cramped muscles Dom climbed gingerly out of the boot, hearing the reticence for his presence he was rightly scared. 'Guys, this is Dom, Dom meet the guys.' Walking over to him Billy was the first to shake his hand, an outstretched arm a welcome sight and a relief to its recipient.

Secondly Nick and Trev approached him, 'welcome mate, good to meet you' they said in unison surveying the cuts and bruises across Doms's face, he really looked like he'd taken a proper pummelling.

Finally, Finn reluctantly came forward 'I'm not sure we can trust you, but if Jase says you're ok I guess that's good enough for me' he grumbled sheepishly.

Greetings aside Jason opened the green door, pretending the creaking noise was coming from his back - once inside the crew scanned the gloom for something to rest on, making a grab for the safest looking chairs before sitting down to an equally rotten looking table in the centre of the room.

The venue was a small, corrugated tin unit originally part of an old farm - being dry, relatively warm, and away from prying eyes it seemed the perfect place to meet covertly to discuss matters in hand.

A hundred yards up the road a shiny black vehicle - the same style and shape to the one previously seen outside the Ship Inn gently pulled up, hiding itself neatly behind some overhanging trees but still providing a good line of sight to the occupants. Inside the car sat two menacing gentlemen, cloaked in body armour, with side arms on both flanks and several other pockets seemingly bristling with knives, ammunition - accompanied by the odd grenade.

The driver picked up the radio 'Charlie One to base, Charlie One to base do you read me, over?'

'Go ahead Charlie One', came an instantaneous reply 'Suspects have arrived, repeat suspects have arrived, over'.

Stood outside Jasons house, team leader Barney Jameson responded, 'OK, Charlie One, stay close, don't intercept we're going in, over.'

'Roger that, Charlie One out.' Putting his radio down and turning to his passenger he moaned 'how come we get to baby sit, I wanna smash stuff up.'

Back at Jasons the order was given and a group of seven equally heavily armed men forced the front door open nearly taking it off its hinges. Running into each room the group each shouted 'clear' as they checked for any occupants. 'Sir' said one of them to his team leader 'the place is empty. I don't know where that Spanish git has gone but he ain't here either.'

'Dammit' came the response, 'check around and see if there's any signs he's been here' - the men immediately started investigating, which seemed to involve more destruction than searching.

Crowded around the table in the farm hut Jason started to speak - 'For every action the government takes there's an underlying agenda, once you see through the charade the truth quickly reveals itself.

Parliamentarians who live in their tax funded cosseted clique are immune to the suffering their policies impose on our nation, although they are not ignorant to the results and still willingly carry them out because there's no detriment to them. MPs have forgotten who they represent, more to the point who employs them - it's time to change the cruel system of government in Great Britain.

General elections don't work because voters have a visceral fear of change and will continue to elect the red and blue tag team that's governed our nation since time immemorial, despite the damage to the fabric of our society.

When party leaders portray more positions than the Karma Sutra as they attempt to garner voter affection, it's plain to see we shouldn't listen to a single word they say.

Any attempt to show a modicum of concern for the interests of the voting public is merely a charade designed to keep the docile, blinkered, servile public on side and in their usual lapdog pose.

You all know what happened to my Sarah, our

beautiful daughter Milly - to Dom's family, and

our friends too - well the simple truth is that

our government is behind it. Tens of

thousands have gone missing in our area

alone. Media outlets across the land aren't

reporting on it, but they seem to be targeting

the middle classes - the management

structure - perhaps the government believes

these folk are unnecessary but if we don't

stick together, we will eventually all be

smashed by the same brick, so to speak.

Billy was right, history has proven that once

they get away with something the government

feel empowered to do more, our inaction is

seen as acceptance with the nation silently

condoning their policies - we need push back, or who knows where this will end up.

For years they have attempted to divide us because they know it makes them stronger'.

Standing tall and strong Jason slapped a book on the table, that he'd borrowed off Billy – Guerrilla Warfare by the revolutionary, Che Guevara.

Veins pumping in his neck from a mixture of anger and excitement he could hardly contain himself as he tried to calmly state - 'having had a fair deal of time to think about this, the most important rules of Guerrilla Warfare are to plan, organise and carry out your attack swiftly, the longer you mess around the more likely you are to get caught, the smaller the

group the better, again you're less likely to get
caught.'

Nick looked startled 'Guerrilla warfare, Jesus
Christ Jason what the hell are you getting us
into, have you gone bloody mad? We can't
just pick up arms and start fighting the
government, we will all be killed'.

'Nick mate, we are being systematically exterminated by this bloody government anyway, we all know Britain is overpopulated and it seems like they've come up with their perfect solution – a nationwide cull. They've been trying to kill the pensioners off for years, we cannot and must not allow them to get away with it.'

Trev stepped in 'Nick, I've been thinking about the current crisis for a while now and I can understand your reservations but to be fair Jase is correct, look at our management team – disappeared, look at Dom's family – disappeared, look at Jasons family – dead as a result of government stooges disappearing another family in Shirley High Street - for God's sake man when will enough be enough? It's clear that we are the carbon they wish to reduce, and they don't care how they do it.'

Taking to his feet Dom interjected shakily, 'your Magna Carta was issuing in June 1215, it state the kings and his el estado - sorry the state, not being above the law – many centuria of manipulation, erosions, coercions, and ignorance on behalf of public has allowing laws created that handed corrupt government ultimate power in interest of security national.

Today, Magna Carta is parchment of empty wording, our leaders out of control and royal ascent given to any laws passed under nosing of weak-willed monarchs afeared of losing state incomes.

Something has to be changing.'

Forgetting their initial lack of trust in the unfamiliar guest, the rest of the team gestured their approval with nods, fascial expressions and the odd 'yep'.

Not wishing to miss an opportunity Billy took his turn 'guys, I'm only an apprentice - as you keep reminding me, just a nipper and I would hope to have a long life ahead of me, but if our so-called leaders wish to cull those, they are supposed to represent then I'm in.

I wouldn't trust the current crop of MPs to house sit when I'm on holiday let alone sit in the Houses of Parliament. They are literally stealing a wage and representing the views of global spin doctors who have no care when it comes to the servile classes.

I've said to you before, remember the Martin Niemöller poem - it's patently obvious that we will be next. If honesty, integrity, and patriotism could be harvested we would reap a very poor crop from Westminster.

Politicians are our employees, and as such need to be sacked, removed, and disposed of.

Guys, the elite strata in our society have declared war on us - and we cannot sit back and accept this violence against humanity.'

Jason wore a wry smile as the depth of support grew, he turned to Finn, 'what do you reckon mate' he said inquisitively?'

Finn responded, 'you know I have a family, I have a life, I have commitments, and I have a decent paying job – however, none of that means feck all if I am not around to appreciate it, so believe it or not lads I'm in - it'll be a craic and I cannot allow the English to have all the glory, especially against the British government, father would turn in his grave, god bless his soul'

All heads turned to Nick; he was shaking as he looked around the table 'I'm in too, but only if I agree the plan is feasible.'

The group cheered, there was a bit of apprehension, a lot of fear but most of all adrenalin pumping through the veins of this intrepid band of revolutionaries.

Old Trev stood up - rubbing his arthritic knees he stated 'if we are going to be successful, we need to get all the MPs in Westminster together, like rats in a barrel, but the lazy swine only turn up when they feel like it, which is why next week's perfect. They will all be voting on their pay rise, so you can guarantee those trough diving pigs will make sure they're all there, it's the only time of year the useless arse-wipes will be, the question is how we do it, Guy Fawkes made a complete botch of it to be honest.'

'That's why we need to keep the group small, act swift and brutal, we need to attack from distance, perhaps with some sort of shoulder launched missile.' Jason responded.

A newly energised Nick turned round and said, 'My mates a militaria collector and has

WW2 PIAT's they're a portable anti-tank launcher that uses a massive spring.'

'Yeah, but unfortunately they only fire for about 150 yards, we need something powerful to hit the buildings with enough force to cause maximum damage.' Finn retorted.

'How about an EFP – an Explosively Formed Penetrator, delivered from a lorry outside of Westminster' suggested Billy hoping to impress. 'This isn't Call of Duty, and I bet your Aunty would notice if you started cooking up something like that in her kitchen' laughed Nick.

'Lads, we work on the docks where there's plenty of military hardware coming through - I know where there's a good stash. The government move arms disguised as goods for their secret interventions in foreign wars, there's hardly any security because no one really knows what it is, and they don't want to attract attention' shouted Billy with a clear sense of excitement.

'Nice one Billy' they all replied, as he sat back down grinning after redeeming himself from his previous comment.

Finn stood up, his huge frame causing the light to obliterated from the room, 'my sister works in St Thomas' Hospital on the South Bank of the Thames, I've been on the roof for a cigarette or two, there's a direct line of site for the Houses of Parliament and Portcullis House next door – that's where the MP's have their offices, if we get some rocket launchers we could hit them both from there, and if we get a chance we could have a pop at the Security Intelligence Services (MI6) just down river to the west.'

'Excellent Finn, sound idea mate' Jason said grinning from ear to ear, their plan was quickly evolving, and revenge was in the air. Grabbing a pen and pad he scribbled a rough map to share with the lads.

Billy continued - 'if we are going to access the roof we can walk straight through the front door wearing high viz vests and overalls – oddly enough wearing an old hi viz doesn't make you stand out, in fact it does the opposite - pushing you into the background, one of those oiks that people don't wish to spark up a conversation with, a silent member

of society that people know are there but

don't wish to associate with, a yellow vest is

like an invisibility cloak.

Add a dirty pair of overalls and society will turn its gaze from you, not wishing to associate with those who fit a social stereotype in their minds eye - leaving us able to boldly walk through reception into the lift - add a clip board and some paperwork and we have a clear pass. One of us can stay in the van waiting for the others to lower the window cleaning basket ready to carry the weapons to the roof undetected.'

'Nice work Billy' Jason replied, 'you worry me sometimes it's as if you've been studying this for some time, I wonder what else is going on in that little head of yours - I think we can all agree that it sounds perfect?'

All those around the table nodded in appreciation, some still looking at the young lad quizzingly wondering what makes him tick. Jason continued - 'the only problem we have is making our escape, any ideas guys?'

Thinking he'd not have anything like Billys contribution Nick surprised himself when he stated 'I can fly a helicopter - there's an air ambulance stationed on the roof of the hospital, and I could fly us out of there...'

The rest of the dockers looked equally astonished 'bloody hell Nick, I didn't expect that mate' Trev responded thankfully, 'it sounds like a plan, what about the MI6 building down river I'm not sure there's an exposed section by direct line of sight, what if we can't hit it?'

Running his finger over the map Billy pointed
to the edge of Security Intelligence Services
building - 'the eastern flank looks as though
we could at least take that section out,
sending the message across social media
that we are not afraid of anyone. With the
internet in mind, I will ensure I have my
computer gear, camera, and the Wi Fi
password for St Thomas' so I can live stream
to the world - creating a catalyst of resistance
to end this autocratic reign.

All previous attempts to form an alliance of
working people have been crushed or vilified
by the vermin who are supposed to represent
us - our actions will hopefully wake people up,
remove their fear, sow the seeds of change,
and encourage a violent struggle, it's our only

option after years of lies, corruption, abuse and forced servility.

To quote Pierre-Joseph Proudhon - to be governed is to be kept in sight, inspected, spied upon, directed, law driven, numbered, enrolled, indoctrinated, preached at, controlled, estimated, valued, censured, and commanded - by creatures who have neither the right, nor the wisdom, nor the virtue to do so.' Billy was in his element, after years of study, posting or arguing with mates, here he

Pierre Proudhon

was, the centre of attention, sharing ideas and controlling the narrative.

He continued quoting one of his favourite sociologists - 'to be governed is to be, at every operation, every transaction, noted, registered, enrolled, taxed, stamped, measured, numbered, assessed, licensed, authorized, admonished, forbidden, reformed, corrected, punished.

It is, under pretext of public utility, and in the name of the general interest, to be placed under contribution, trained, ransacked, exploited, monopolized, extorted, squeezed, mystified, robbed; then, at the slightest resistance, the first word of complaint, to be repressed, fined despised, harassed, tracked, abused, clubbed, disarmed, choked, imprisoned, judged, condemned, shot, deported, sacrificed, sold, betrayed; and, to crown all, mocked, ridiculed, outraged, dishonoured.

That is government; that is its justice; that is its morality.'

Taking a breath at last he looked around the room proudly, surveying his newfound fanbase who seemed to appreciate the passionate outburst.

'Bloody hell lads, Vive La Révolution, aye Billy' - Jason said slapping him on the back laughing with him, 'great work son, you've found your true vocation, now lads have we missed anything?'

An approving mumble and shaking of heads confirmed that his band of guerrillas were ready, willing, and able.

Let's spend the next couple of days working out whose doing what and look at getting access to these weapons.'

Walking outside, the group felt invigorated by their meeting, positive they could, and would succeed.

As he got used to the light a glint in the distance caught Jason's eye - 'guys I think we have company' Jase could see the same vehicle that appeared to be following him around, 'let's get ourselves gone and catch up tomorrow.'

The officers radio came to life with a loud boom from Barney Jameson 'Charlie One, suspects nowhere to be seen, intercept Bailey, repeat intercept Bailey, don't let the villainous bastard get away - I know he's up to something, over'.

Before the team leader could even finish talking a helicopter burst through the clouds flying noisily overhead, the black cars wheels span as it launched across the narrow bridge and the group dispersed in all directions, Dominguez jumped into Betsi as she catapulted up the road - the lane was difficult to navigate but Jason was familiar with the area.

'Hang on buddy' he said roaring round a tight bend 'this used to be an even higher jump

167

until they flattened it out' - the car flew skywards as the rear wheels span in mid-air before the yellow beast came firmly down on the tarmac, sparks flew in all directions as the rear differential, sump and suspension clouted the road surface at 70mph.

Tearing round the next bend Jason floored it before yanking the hand brake and sliding through a right-hand turn. Betsi's wheels smoked, and her engine growled as he took the roundabout the wrong way, shooting towards the M271 before darting up a side road. Jason flicked immediately the lights off to conceal themselves and slowed down to a more moderate pace.

Dominguez loosened his grip on the handholds, his fingers white and brow

168

dripping with sweat - 'that was some driving there compadre, more comfortable than boot.'

Meanwhile Billy and the rest of the group had arrived on foot so jumped the adjacent gate and fled into the neighbouring paintball centre - rapidly dispersing through the fields and woods at the rear of the premises the renegades looked set to get away.

Nick and Finn disappeared into the night as Billy glanced back to see Trev leaning on the rear fence puffing and panting surrounded by guards, the poor old fella wasn't as spritely as the rest and he'd been caught - arthritic knees don't do well in sprints, moreover an overweight body works like a handbrake preventing a car picking up any kind of speed.

The young lad stopped, turned, and ran back towards his stricken workmate before athletically vaulting the fence and diving behind a hedge. 'This is like a war game' he thought to himself crawling along the ground inside the perimeter - looking across to his right he could see a whole batch of freshly loaded paintball guns laid out ready for the following day's events.

Creeping slowly behind the counter he could hear the guards berating poor Trev - 'you silly old git, you couldn't walk to the burger van, let alone run away from us' said one, before kicking the old man firmly in the stomach causing him to drop to the floor grimacing.

Billys neck went red with anger as he grabbed two of the guns - slinging one over his shoulder he charged forward shouting 'LEAVE HIM ALONE' whilst firing pellets straight into the shocked men's privates, the brightly coloured splats bringing a whole new meaning to decorated officer.

They screamed and reeled on the floor in excruciating pain, the stinging sensation ten times worse than any STD and about as bloody welcome.

Billy tore forward firing more liquid bullets - turning their black uniforms blue around the crotch, before casting the empty gun aside and adding some vivid yellow for good measure.

A startled Trev had risen to his feet and with Billys help began trundling into the field. '

That was awesome' chuckled Billy as the duo reached the safety of the adjacent marshes.

'Thanks fella' said a grateful Trev, 'you saved my life there boy, and I'll never forget that.'

'No worries, Trev, we're mates - that's what we do......'

EPISODE 10 – That Sinking Feeling

Across town near Jasons house the other revolutionary pair sat silently enjoying the sound of the engine as the lovely yellow escort purred along.

Turning the corner at the end of his road Jase was shocked to see a fleet of black vans and military goons hanging around outside his property. 'They looking for Dominguez' said Dom sheepishly 'sorry amigo, I draw you to something deeper.'

'Deeper, we're going to blow the bleeding government up, it doesn't get much deeper than that mush - let's get out of here before they see us, I reckon we'd better dump Betsi,

she's slightly conspicuous. '

Driving towards the river Jason stroked the

dashboard saying one last goodbye to his

beloved machine – as they drew up next to

the water Jason stepped out and gave Betsi a

quick shove before watching her sink below

the surface.

'They've killed my wife, they've killed my daughter and now my bloody car - these bastards are going to pay, I can assure you of that my friend.'

Pulling his phone from his pocket Jason called Trev to explain the situation and let him know he wouldn't be at work in the morning, before launching the device into the river too - 'we can't use mobiles anymore as they will be able to triangulate the signal and trace us, luckily enough I have some cash, so we won't leave a credit card trail either.'

'Arrepentido,amigo, sorry about car, she was lovely ride, and Wife and kid - not the ride bit, definitely not the ridings in relations to wife and kid' he said anxiously digging a deeper hole for himself - Jason laughed and put his arm around Dom's shoulder, 'you're a funny guy, I'm glad to have made your acquaintance, now let's go and grab a Pizza I'm starving.'

An hour or so later two figures came out of the night, the bright luminescence of the dockside lights shining down relentlessly on the port like a dessert sun. The pizza filled men snuck in and around the high piles of containers looking for a place to shelter - luckily enough most dock workers knew the best places to disappear for a while.

The pals paused before running across the open stretch of concrete and diving into an old store - 'this will do us for the night, now let's get some sleep it's going to be a long day tomorrow Dom'.

Nestling down amongst some old boxes the troublesome twosome started to slip into slumber, Dominguez gazed at the spiders' webs coating the decrepit ceiling whilst he pondered what's to become of him, would he make it, what would happen after the attack, how would they get away – moreover, did life really matter, when life without his family didn't really seem worth living?

His thoughts waned as he drifted in and out of sleep, until a rustling caught his ear, 'what the hell that' he whispered to himself trying to see in the darkened room.

The rustling stopped, he felt uneasy but was

sufficiently tired for his eyes to close and his

head tilted back into the card-based bed.

Five filthy, frightful, furtive rats emerged from a pile of rubbish in the corner, scurrying silently from hiding place to crevice looking for a bite to eat. Their large teeth revealed themselves in the moonlight as their noses twitched trying to locate the scent of food. The largest of the group was a battle worn fella parading a half-chewed ear and ragged bald patches where skin had been gorged from his body during a rival gang's attack.

Stealthily he made his way across the floor, avoiding discarded drinks cans, for fear of blowing his cover.

Presently, the covert creature found a small pile of seeds hidden under Jason's coat, nudging its nose gently it managed to get a mouthful before his adversaries noticed and began diving in squeaking and squealing as they fought for a share.

Jason woke with a start quickly followed by Dom who had a large rat running up his torso trying to escape the mele, the air became filled with swearing and cursing in English and Spanish as the panic-stricken duet strived to get the rats away from themselves.

'Jase, getting this thing off me - filthy alimaña she in my hairs.'

Picking up a broom Jason swung it around before pushing the huge rat off Dom's head.

It was difficult to know who was more scared the rodent invaders or the flailing docker and his mate - fortunately for the latter the rodents made a hasty getaway, squealing into the darkness and out the hole they'd entered from.

'Jesús Jase, I thought I was going to the death.'

Across the darkened room Jason laughed 'I think we've got bigger things than them to worry about - but just as verminous, let's see if we can get some sleep.' Dominguez didn't look too confident about the last statement as he would - without doubt be keeping one eye open for the rest of the night.......

EPISODE 11 – Getting the Gear

The following morning both men looked dishevelled - 'I'm off to steal some work clothes so I can blend in and meet up with Trev, stay here and keep an eye out, Dom - don't worry, I think our furry friends have gone, it's a shame really you could have had a couple for breakfast'.

Dom looked down at his grumbling stomach but shook his head as Jase snuck out the door.

Donning some discarded safety gear, Jason strolled across the docks - nobody would really notice him amongst the hustle and bustle, especially as they wouldn't know he'd gone missing after last night's events.

Closing in on where Trev worked, he could see the Forman talking to the lads in his team. 'Where the hell is he' Jimmy growled with clear hostility in his voice, 'we are short staffed already without losing more - if you see him tell the useless git to get his arse in gear and come to see me at tea break, I've had the Police in my office this morning, I don't know what he's got himself involved in but they seem keen to find him - and I won't put up with any more of his crap.'

Trev raised his finger 'you've changed your sodding tune haven't you Jim, stepping into a supervisory role has somehow turned you into bloody Stalin - Jase is a decent guy he's been through the mill lately and arseholes like you don't make it any easier for him - I expected better from you.'

Realising the loss of respect Jimmy shouted, 'I'm the bloody foreman - you're just a grunt'

He then stuck his middle finger up at Trev, before barking 'so you can get back to work before I can your arse too, you fat useless fat git.'

Trev lunged forward but Finn held him back - 'that maggot isn't worth it pal, just let it go, we've got bigger fish to fry and cannot let that jumped-up bag of piss get in the way of things.'

Reluctantly turning the other cheek, they started to walk towards the neighbouring piles of containers before noticing Jase waving his arm - indicating for them to come over.

'Alright lads' he greeted them - 'the filth have trashed my house, me and Dom had to leg it and dump Betsi in the river last night, we've been hiding out in the old store on the end of row B.'

'Bleeding hell Jase, the garda haven't rumbled us, have they?' asked Finn in a perturbed voice - the concern slightly masked by his bushy red beard.

'Nah them lot couldn't catch a cold - I reckon they thought I was just shielding Dom, they obviously chased me last night, but I doubt they knew what I was doing at the meeting or who else was there. We need to move quickly

before they put two and two together -
where's Billy?

'No problem, Jase he's working with me
tonight' replied Trev – 'it gets dark around
1800 hrs, and we're both staying late due to
staffing issues, where shall we meet you
fella?'

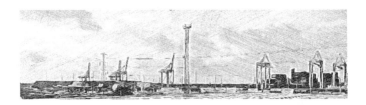

'Over by the corner of row sixty-seven mush,
I'll bring a van' he responded before slinking
off into the shadowy avenues of shipping
containers forming a multi-coloured,
corrugated vista - reminiscent of an old paint

chart and in some ways quite artistic, in a modern industrialist kind of way.

Later that evening Jason and Dominguez strolled through the vast dock's storage yard 'won't anyone be seeing us Jase, we in the openings here, anyone can see us.'

Jason responded calmly 'don't worry mate - because the docks have security at the main entrance people believe the whole thing is a secure compound and anyone inside must be kosher, the keys to the vans will be just inside the building over there.

I will sign a van out for a few days and by the time anyone notices we will be long gone, wait here by the door and give me a shout if anyone's coming – there's so many new staff due to the disappearance's that I doubt anyone will question you.'

Jason nipped inside the vacant office and began filling in the forms - smiling to himself he put his name down as Jimmy Drago the annoying foreman, before taking the keys and exiting the building.

'Right my friend lets grab our wheels and meet up with Billy and Trev'.

After waiting until just before 0200 hrs Jason drove the van to their rendezvous - early morning is the night shifts lunchtime, meaning security wouldn't be staring aimlessly at their cameras - making it the perfect time to implement their cunning plan.

Pulling up on the corner of row sixty-seven their partners in crime appeared from the shadows like a pair of cat burglars - little and large strolled forward in all their glory, stinky oversized overalls with shredding trouser bottoms dragging along the concrete surface

– proving one size doesn't fit all - poor Billy looked like he was swimming in his suit and his hardhat sat jauntily at an angle smothering his head. After years of use their Hi-Viz vest wasn't particularly visible - but to be fair being noticed wasn't on the agenda.

'Alright boys, hop in - where are we going?' came a call from the van. Settling himself on top of an old wooden box behind the cab Billy pointed straight ahead - 'we are looking for container 553 ZDY, it should be green and located on the lower level and on the left-hand side'.

The headlights lit up the gloom as the quartet mouthed the numbers out like pretend singers in a church - soon they could see the container, its green paint shining out like a beacon of hope ready to relinquish its stockpile of arms to fight the good fight and release the nation from its fascist grip.

Three of the gang jumped from the van, followed more cautiously by Trev - recognising his old pins weren't suitable for athleticism anymore and required a more sedate approach.

Gathered in anticipation at the front of the container they stared at Billy's bolt croppers as he offered them up to the lock - 'well here goes' he said hoping the payload was inside.

With a satisfying clump the cutter easily sliced the solid steel with as much resistance as a block of Cheddar, before the lock dropped to the floor missing Trev's foot by a couple of inches, 'steady now Billy - you're lucky I've got my toecaps on' he said smiling at the young lad before grasping the handle and swinging the door open.

It was like a pirates haul inside with guns, ammunition and militaria hiding in the shadows, 'Jesus Christ Billy, you're an absolute star, a frigging genius, how the hell you knew I won't ask - but well done you' whispered a happy Jason.

After creeping around in the darkened box Trev called out 'I've found them, there's at least eighteen rocket launchers here, packed neatly in boxes of three, we may as well take a couple of stun grenade crates for luck.'

The group formed a line, passing each unit swiftly between each other into the back of the waiting van. Once safely stowed Jase called out 'nice one guys – Trev and Billy get yourselves back to work before anyone notices, me and Dom will head out of the docks and meet up tomorrow – well done again Billy, it's great to have you on board.'

The young man beamed contentedly, for the first time in his life he felt part of something.

Clamping a new lock and plastic tab on the container, to avoid suspicion they climbed back into the vehicle and drove off into the night - revolution was in the air.

Approaching the security hut at Dock Gate 20 Jason remarked - 'don't worry the guards are on minimum wage, he won't step out.'

How wrong could he be - some security operatives take their jobs seriously, seeing it as an opportunity to utilise combat experience gained in conflicts across the globe - this was one of those occasions.

A smartly dressed man stepped out from the warmth of his booth waving a clip board - as if it was going to stop anyone, the van accelerated but the guard belligerently refused to allow Jason to exit without the obligatory formal checks being carried out.

Inside the cab the two men grimaced as they sped through the gate. The security guard jumped, then yelped as he bounced off the side of the van - his clip board flying through the night sky followed by his neatly preened hat.

Thumping to the floor in an untidy pile of flailing limbs he shouted - 'you arseholes, you'll pay for this.'

Jason looked in mirror the man was standing up - so not too badly damaged, 'prancock' he said shaking his head in the wing mirror as they hurtled across the bridge towards the roundabout - 'he'll feel that in the morning, the dopey git.'

With its wheels spinning wildly the van flew through the green traffic lights onto, and around the roundabout, 'blimey green light…… luck is on our side – but to be fair

that reminds me of another reason to get rid

of the current crop of cretins in Westminster,

who'd put lights on roundabouts 24 hours a

day - causing traffic jams, wasting electricity,

wasting my fuel - then claim they are being

green - bloody idiots……'

EPISODE 12 – The Execution

Dominguez slunk low in the van seat looking furtively around Mayflower Park as he waited for his pal - Jason sat on a swing revisiting memories of happier times with his wife and family, 'come on amigo' he muttered to himself - his complexion red and forehead sweaty giving him the appearance of someone carrying out bomb disposal rather than a man waiting in a van.

Jase looked morose, with a furrowed brow, teary eyes and shaking hands he mumbled sweet words of love for the dearly departed girls he'd devoted himself to before they were torn from him by the demonic actions of the British Government.

Staring across the river his mind began to cloud, the pressure gave him the feeling of falling and spinning, a metallic taste appeared in his mouth followed by a red mist in both eyes.

Remembering the words from social media 'If we all become a pouting bottom lip republic devoid of any resistance other than moaning into the froth on our beer's humanity is lost and we may as well be amoeba aimlessly floating in the waters of life' - he convinced himself he was doing the right thing.

'My darling girls I miss you so much, you were my life and my reason for being, now I must avenge your passing, wake up the nation and take our country back - no matter the cost.'

Jason released two kisses from his hand and marched towards the van, Dominguez looked relieved - 'hurrying, hurrying' he mouthed, signalling his mate to get back in the van before the authorities saw them.

About an hour later a newly calm Dom opened the rusty old roller shutter door of an abandoned warehouse unit nestled amongst open farmland north of the city, the kind of place that urbex crews would love to explore, filming themselves sifting through abandoned cabinets and masses of defunct machinery nestled amongst a bed of cobwebs, nettles and ivy waiting for nature to reclaim them.

Jason quickly drove the van into its new hiding place before immediately jumping out shouting - 'thank Christ for that, I'm busting for a piss' as he ran across the dusty concrete floor to a stench filled toilet that looked like it hadn't been flushed for years. The acrid smell of stale urine caught the back of his throat causing him to cough the unwelcome rank air from his lungs.

'Frigging hell Dom, I don't think anyone's gonna disturb us here – the place is an absolute hole.'

Dom and Jase laughed as the surveyed their

temporary home. The asbestos roof looked

proper dodgy, the steel frame had certainly seen better days and the gardener must have been absent for decades, but as Jason said nobody would bother them in the short time they would be there.

Over recent days Finn had been stockpiling some gear enabling the crew to have all the appearance of air conditioning engineers to meet with their planned excuse to access the hospital roof.

Racking on either side of the wall was loaded with overalls, high viz vests, air conditioning service equipment and various power tools preassembled in readiness for the big day - he'd even had some stickers made up for the side of the van 'Grants Conditioning' would be

emblazoned across its flanks, a nod towards
the removal of their demonic Prime Minister.

Taking the military storage cases from the
back of the van the two new pals started to
prepare them for paint - 'we've gotta disguise
these things as plumbing equipment or
material containers so the law won't become
suspicious if they look in the back of the van -
we'll get these done then have a kip before
the rest turn up in the morning.'

Dom looked up. 'Sounding like plan Jase, let's
getting the moving - I'm absolutely cansado,
long days.'

Grabbing a couple of rattle cans Dom
vigorously shook them to thoroughly mix their
contents before randomly spraying a deep

blue colour onto the crate in front of him -
dispelling the urban myth 'if you can piss you
can paint'.

'Sodding hell mate - that looks awful' said
Jase laughing his head off as pigmented sags
glistened in the evening light - 'you'd make a
crap graffiti artist; you've got more runs than a
curry addicts' arse.'

Dom's face creased as a beaming smile
appeared across it - 'I'll be loaded the gear in
van, you finishing the painting, much safer
that way, I'm knowing limits' he chuckled
whilst placing an array of maintenance
materials in the waiting vehicle.

The following morning shards of light beamed
through gaps in the buildings structure acting

like an unwelcome alarm clock - 'what is el tiempo amigo?' - Jason rubbed his eyes, gave a deep yawn revealing his extensive dental work before replying '6am fella, the rest of the lads should be here shortly.'

Almost immediately a rotten wooden side door burst open smacking into the crumbling brick work - 'morning ladies' shouted someone much too happy at silly o'clock in the morning.

'Bloody hell Finn' complained a dusty Jase picking himself up from the floor - 'I crapped myself you pillock, I thought it was the filth kicking the door in, you daft bugger.'

'Sorry lad's' said Finn, looking as sheepish a six foot plus giant can when they're grinning like a schoolchild, 'I'm just buzzing to send a rocket up their British backsides - can't wait mate.'

'No worries fella, welcome to terrorist central – the van's loaded and ready to go, did you bring anything for breckie?'

Finn smiled as he passed a crumpled wrapper to his mate - 'vegan platter for two' he jested.

'That's not even funny' Jason responded - making pretend reaching noises as he waved a pair of fingers inside his mouth before finding a pair of bacon, sausage and egg rolls cosseted in the light embrace of the small brown bag before him, 'thanks mate, I knew you weren't that much of a git' he said laughing before diving in to grab his much needed rations - 'here you go Dom, get that down your neck son - proper grub.'

Within an hour the rest of the crew had arrived and were busily donning their boiler suits and Hi-Viz - the mood was buoyant with excitement, adrenaline had invigorated the crew as they cast aside any feeling of tiredness, today was the day they would enact their revenge for all those who'd had their lives destroyed by the cull.

'Right guys, we are going to take the A3, there's not so many police patrols on that road, Finn has fitted new plates to our van replicating another one from the storage yard - due to our slight indiscretion with the security guard last night, we don't want to provide any reason for the police to sniff around. Everyone must keep their heads down in the back, and make sure the explosives are tightly rigged – you know what I'm like on roundabouts......'

Sometime later the newly appointed NHS maintenance crew pulled up outside St Thomas' Hospital across the river from the halls of power. Jason and Finn hopped out along with Dom, Nick, and Trev - 'Billy, please stay in the van fella, sit in the driver's seat and explain to anyone who asks that you are waiting to unload, they're normally pretty good with tradesmen.'

Billy looked slightly disappointed but to some degree grateful for having an easy escape should things turn south with the plan.

The others donned a baseball cap to shield their faces from the cameras before entering the sliding doors at reception - tramping purposefully with clipboard in hand and pen behind an ear the gang quickly made their way to the elevators, receiving directions from Finn as they went.

Gathered in the lift Dom whispered - 'no talkings, no look up these lifts are camera by security.'

Eventually a welcome ding, followed by a silky voice welcomed them to the top floor adjacent to the roof access.

A heavy-set fire door was the only barrier to them accessing the roof, each step seemed to take forever as they made their way up the staircase before gingerly pushing the exit bar and releasing themselves onto the waiting surface.

'Bleeding hell, we did it' Nick cried in disbelief, as he and the others scanned the huge expanse around them.

Across the river Parliament loomed ominously from the banks of the River Thames, it looked resplendent with its gothic architecture and spires punching the sky accompanied by a beautifully rippled image reflecting in the still waters below - a stark contrast to the evil residing inside.

'Don't romanticise too much about the beautiful vision before you - we have a job to do and we all know why, let's get this window cleaning cage into position and lower it down to Billy before he falls asleep.'

Sitting comfortably behind the steering wheel Billys face changed, he could see a Policeman walking towards him attempting to make eye contact - the young man raised his hand to wave and try to look unconcerned.

'Afternoon sonny, what's going on here then?' the officer enquired in a kindly voice - 'hello sir, I'm just waiting for the rest of the crew to lower the cage down, so we can do some emergency repairs to the aircon on the hospital roof, I'm really sorry if we've caused any trouble?' replied Billy with a new grown confidence - lying seemed to come all too naturally to him.

The Policeman looked down – 'you are on double yellow lines son, are you able to move this thing to a more appropriate position?'

Billy thought for a second - 'I'm sorry sir, I don't have a driver's licence and am only sitting here to keep the van from being stolen,' looking up he could see the cage approaching rapidly with Finn smiling down like a huge ape enjoying the ride. 'The cage is here officer, please would it be Ok to load up, then move off – it is somewhat of an emergency, the patients are becoming extremely uncomfortable in the heat?'

The kindly constable looked up, looked at him, looked at the van with its sign written side then responded, 'OK sonny - just make it quick, we need to keep these thoroughfares free for emergency units, you know?'

'Thanks sir - we will do' responded Billy politely, doing his best to look like an adolescent angel.

With a loud clang Finn arrived on the pavement, hopped out and began grabbing gear from the van - 'everything all right, mate?' he asked – 'yes fella, the copper only wanted to warn us to keep the road clear, I reckon he won't be too much trouble, especially when we give him and his colleague's a minor distraction shortly' Billy said laughing.

On the roof Trev busied himself by sealing off the access doors with his trusty battery drill -

he clamped them shut with several sturdy six-inch screws before attaching a core drill to make a large circular hole in the stairway roof, Jason looked puzzled - 'grenade holes to deter anyone from attacking via the fire exit,' responded Trev.

Jase nodded approvingly, it would seem his crew had guts and brains - a good combination when up against the full power of the government's enforcement officers.

Whilst Billy set up the livestream camera and Wi-Fi feed the rest of the renegades quickly unloaded the window cleaner's basket, laying out the rockets primed and in position to fire at the various targets.

Finn paused to look at his watch - 'It's 1400 hrs, them langers will be gathering inside ready to vote - Billy check out the BBC Parliament channel and shout when the place is brimming.'

The Air Ambulance glistened in the sun, it's bright red and yellow satisfyingly fresh livery must be a welcome sight for those in peril – however, the peril was going to be slightly different today as it ferried a group of escaping rebels to safety.

Nick sat in the pilot's seat examining the layout and familiarising himself with the controls, it's keys were in the ignition, the fuel gauge was full, and all seemed right with the world, 'she's a gooden Jase, we'll soar out of here in no time - that's for sure.'

They both strolled back to the edge of the roof

as Billy shouted that Parliament was full -

whilst he made exploding gestures with his

hands and explosive noises with his mouth.

'OK boys, we're on' shouted Jase - they all

gathered into a pre match circle and gave

each other a big hug - 'let's do this thing, it's

time to free our nation' they all crowed confidently.

Oblivious to their pending doom the MPs crammed themselves into the chamber - for the first time in twelve months the hall was full, like a sea of rats clambering over each other to ensure they could be seen by the speaker who sat in his chair glibly waiting for the foregone conclusion that another 25% would be added to the already inflated salaries of the throng before him.

From the benches Bill Blackburn's voice boomed across the floor - 'gentlemen, and ladies of course, we are gathered here today with view to voting for the pay rise on offer - and I for one don't wish to appear greedy but the amount of work I do each year, the sacrifices I've made for our nation and the deep felt love I have for my constituents surely deserves this token gesture as a reflection of Great Britain's gratitude towards me, I mean this assembly.

My god, those pernicious plebs wouldn't be able to survive if it wasn't for our endeavours, what do you think PM?' Standing up smugly and trying to be heard over the cheers filling the house Prime Minister Grant adjusted his collar, stood firmly upright and shouted - 'I couldn't agree more, we're solving the housing crisis more rapidly than anyone could have ever expected, our recycling figures are off the scale whilst the economy is booming after cutting the fat of wasteful middle management jobs - this is what voters have been hankering for.

We as a collective should be proud of what we have achieved for these snotty, bothersome ingrates and they should be grateful to us.

25% is merely a morsal, we are not greedy people, we are not ignorant, we understand it may seem generous to some but in all honesty the politics of jealousy should have been put to bed a long time ago - I propose we accept this gesture and look forward to hearing the thoughts of our learned friend opposite.'

Democracy had died in this house decades ago when both government and opposition adopted identical policies, positions and aims.

As the theatre of pretend debate continued inside Westminster the crew across the river were ready to send their gesture to the repulsive assembly - donning balaclavas the revolutionary band looked towards Billy who started live-streaming, as he took his position.

Jase shouted 'FIVE – FOUR – THREE – TWO - ONE – FIRE.'

In unison a flock of missiles flew steadfastly towards their targets, a stream of fire roaring from the rear of each launcher - as quickly as the first rockets left, the crew grabbed the next sending them concurrently target bound.

The first hits struck the roof and front walls of Parliament, a huge explosion tearing the ancient structure apart before Big Ben took a direct blow to its midriff. Parts of Portcullis House flew into the air as the sky filled with bright orange and red shards.

Further down river the MI6 building took two massive blasts on its flank - just as predicted they couldn't destroy the whole building, but the message was strong.

The deed was done - the lads stood back in

awe as the halls of power came tumbling

down.

Inside there were screams from all directions as Parliamentary representatives clambered over each other in a cockroach-esq display, old oak timbers came crashing down on a startled Prime Minister - 'what the hell is going on?' he cried as his clothes caught fire and pain seared through his whole body.

Bills fat filled carcass sizzled as it provided

plenty of fuel for the blazing fire. All entrances

were blocked by burning rubble and blazing

roofing - the MP's had to face the fact their

political careers where over.

The internet had gone mad - the live stream was already being viewed by over 5 billion people worldwide.

Throughout the whole structure flames cleansed the halls of power - removing any last trace of the vicious governors inside - they'd had their chance, they'd had they're warnings, but they'd failed to heed any of them, instead their arrogance had led to their extermination and an opportunity for a fresh start for the United Kingdom.

EPISODE 13 – The Great Escape

Opposite the burning hulk, the cheering and dancing ended abruptly on the hospital roof as the explosive sound of ordnance burst from the stairwell door, a spray of bullets splintered through its red wood face peppering the timber with smoking holes.

Trev immediately grabbed a stun grenade and dropped it through his precut hole in the roof, followed with two more as the strike force scattered below - the sound of metal clattering down the stairs preceded a huge explosion that rang out leaving reeling bodies in the hallway.

Billy gathered the computer gear into his bag and ran across the rooftop.

'Let's get the hell out of here' Nick shouted running towards the helicopter - Trevor taped three pairs of stun grenades together and threw each in turn down the waiting hole.

Before they had a chance to detonate a shot rang out catching Trev in the shoulder - 'BOLLOCKS' he shouted crumpling to the floor, Finn sped over, scooped the old fella up and threw him over his shoulder like a baby, before running to the waiting helicopter - its rotors now spinning at full speed.

Hearing a large cohort of militia coming up the stairs Billy grabbed another couple of grenades attempting to give the others time to escape, 'get yourselves gone guys, I'm taking the cleaners cage, it's the only way – this lot will be at the door any second.'

Jason looked shocked and sad in equal measure; he didn't want' to leave Billy behind but knew the consequences of not doing so.

Frenzied bullets started to destroy the door, stray rounds hit the helicopters shining paint job as shell casings tinkled down the stairs - the young revolutionary caught one in the leg and was now writhing on the floor.

'BILLY' shouted Jason - 'BILLY, GET THE HELL OUT OF THERE.'

As the brave apprentice raised himself from the floor grimacing in pain, the door flung open but with the bowl of an expert cricketer he lobbed a grenade through the entrance sending the occupants scattering.

After the explosion more shots were fired hitting the rear rotor on the waiting means of escape, 'Jase get the hell off the roof, I'm going in the basket, now GO!!!' Billy cried as he stumbled over to the edge, released a couple more grenades before dropping into the cage, immediately pressing to go down and disappearing vertically as the last of the explosives went off, sending deafening thunderclaps in all directions.

Nick pulled on the helicopters controls and flew the damaged chopper skywards before rotor failure caused it to immediately lurch downwards, smash through the avenue of trees and crash into the soft green turf on the other side of the park, leaving a trail of thick

black smoke behind.

Dragging themselves from the wreckage the

hero's looked up to face three-armed

response officers pointing automatic rifles

directly at them - 'ON THE FLOOR' the leader

shouted before kicking Finn to the ground.

'You wouldn't do that if you didn't have a gun

you gobshite' Finn snarled back at him.

'Well, I do have a gun, meat head so stay the hell down if you know what's good for you.'

Billy was having the same amount of luck - the response units had made their way to the roof and were firing downwards, trying to put some holes in the intrepid lad - who was now hanging underneath the cradle to shield himself from the hail of ammunition.

The platform above him took strike after strike from the determined roof-bound troop - the steel sheet looking increasingly like the skin of a freshly plucked chicken.

Looking towards the pavement he could see the friendly Policeman looking up at him about fifteen feet below - feeling a bit guilty for what he was about to do Billy shouted

'SORRY' before letting go and rapidly dropping onto his awaiting cushioned landing.

The poor officer lay flat on his back as the docker jumped into his awaiting van trying to avoid being perforated - fighting the pain in his leg he slammed the vehicle into gear and stormed forward towards his captured pals.

Ting, Ting, Ting went the bullets on the roof as he gathered pace and approached the stricken crew - Jase looked out the corner of his eye - clocking the van he smiled at the smug sods before him as Billy performed a beautifully executed hand brake turn, slamming the van into the enforcement officers and scattering them across the grass.

One smashed his head into the rotor blade,
the other impaled himself on shard of steel
and the last one broke his jaw when Finn
walked over to kick him in the face – 'there,
you little bollocks, you aren't so big anymore
are you.' a vengeful Finn grunted.

Jason turned to Billy - 'thanks mate, you really
are something else, we all owe you, now let's
get out'a here.'

Heading towards the beckoning road Billy
floored the hole pocked machine like he'd
stolen it - although to be fair they had.

'Don't worry lads' Jason said calmly 'London
is 200 square miles of real estate; the Police
couldn't find their own wallets let alone an
individual van amongst so many driving down

the road' - the crew sat silently grinning;

mission accomplished.

EPISODE 14 – The End?

The following morning Jason walked through Southampton cemetery gazing at the beckoning graves.

Kneeling betwixt the headstones of his heaven bound Sarah and Milly Jase softly stroked their glistening monuments muttering 'my darling family, I miss you so much - we've avenged your deaths, but I still feel empty and alone.'

Mopping his tear-soaked cheeks he continued - 'I figured I'd feel better now - it's going to be a struggle but given time perhaps I will come to terms with it.

My mates are with me, so I won't be alone, don't worry my beautiful girls – I love you both but it's time to go, for now.

We must continue our mission; the world is changing rapidly - and someone needs to keep an eye on things.' Kissing his fingers before placing them gently on each stone Jason rejoined his fellow outlaws, turned north, and strolled into the shadows with his hexad - bonded by circumstance some widowed, all homeless and jobless, but each commonly fuelled by a lust for retribution and justice.